THE BUTTERNUT TREE

A COMING-OF-AGE NOVEL, SET IN THE 1940S AND 1950S, BASED UPON A TRUE STORY OF AN UNSPEAKABLE CRIME

THE BUTTERNUT TREE

A COMING-OF-AGE NOVEL, SET IN THE 1940S AND 1950S, BASED UPON A TRUE STORY OF AN UNSPEAKABLE CRIME

BY

MAUREEN ANN RICHARDS KOSTALNICK

www.bookstandpublishing.com

Published by
Bookstand Publishing
Morgan Hill, CA 95037
3678_2

DISCLAIMER

This is a fictional story based on actual events. While many incidents recorded in this book did occur, any resemblance to locales, identifying details or persons (living or nonliving) is entirely coincidental.

ISBN 978-1-61863-318-7

Printed in the United States of America

DEDICATION AND ACKNOWLEDGEMENTS

Written to ensure that these bittersweet memories will live forever: The warm summer days of my Butternut Tree, St. Mary's, Bauers's Pond, and Billy, suspended in time. I wish a Butternut Tree for every troubled child born under the Blessed Mother's heaven.

This book is dedicated to my family: To Chuck, my forever sweetheart; and Kathie, Chuck, and Daniel Jon -- this book is for you. A legacy for my grandchildren: Kaitlin, Taylor, Chuck, Mike, Elizabeth, and twins Madeleine and Danielle are truly God's greatest blessings for this grandmother. You are the family I always prayed for...and more.

Mother, your courage and love got us through every day of our young lives.

For you, Donna, my sister, only a child yourself, when you took on the responsibility of our family.

Brothers Ted and Tommy...Ted, you gave me the internal fortitude to write; Tommy, you still make me laugh. And don't forget,

I did "get you last." I love you with all my heart.

Your Boguidie forever.

A Muchness Of Love

-- Maureen

Very, Very Special Thanks to Kathleen Antrim -- Author, Friend, and Daughter. I could not have done this without you.

Love You Tons,

Mom

For all of you bad

Cause you're sad kids.

You know who you are.

You can stay stuck

Or follow your star.

Trouble at home.

Trouble at school.

Life's not fair.

Life can be cruel.

Show who you *really* are

And who you are not.

Heal your hurt by

Giving what you never got.

How do I know this to be true?

A very long time ago, I was you.

-- Maureen

A NOTE FROM THE AUTHOR

Most of the events in this story take place in the 1940s and 1950s. As a result, I wanted to evoke the feel and atmosphere of that very different, bygone era to the maximum extent possible. I have done so not only with the descriptions set forth herein, drawing upon my own memories and experiences from back then, but by making the book physically reminiscent of a typewritten document that could have originated in that time. To that end, I have set the book in the Courier New typeface, which nicely evokes typewritten text.

Perhaps this is appropriate for another reason as well: When I began writing this book some twenty years ago, I used not a computer, but my old Remington typewriter -- and so my early manuscript was, indeed, typewritten. I hope you agree that this lends an additional air of authenticity to my story.

-- Maureen

PROLOGUE

Avon, Ohio, 1928

A huge hand covered Laura's mouth.

"Scream and I'll slit your throat."

The stranger spat the words into her terrified face. His hand moved from her mouth to a death grip around her throat. She could barely breathe as he forced her down on her back. Laura's eyes darted to the back seat of the black sedan. She could see Gracie lying motionless on the back seat as the other thug ripped off her clothes.

"Please let us go," she managed to choke out.

His eyes flashed with excitement in the near dark of the parking lot. The loud music of Jimmy Dorsey's band filled the dance hall and spilled outside.

"Oh, I'll let you go all right."

He pinned her down on the front seat and brutally raped her.

# # #

Laura awoke in the pouring rain to find herself lying in the gutter of a street in the industrial area of Lakewood, Ohio. She felt like she had been ripped apart inside. Her head swam in the early morning light as she struggled to her feet.

Blood gushed down her legs and swirled in the fast-flowing street water. A gut-wrenching vomiting attack doubled her over in pain.

Screams pulsated in her ears. It was Gracie.

"Laura, I'm sorry! Oh my God!" She was sobbing. "They seemed so nice...We needed a ride home, that's why I told you I knew them!"

Their arms wrapped around each other's waists for support, the two friends wandered the streets until a patrolling policeman found them.

This was only a slice of the testimony given in court by Gracie, one of the teenaged victims. Her friend, Laura, was in a mental asylum undergoing electroconvulsive therapy -- shock treatment -- and was unable to testify. The mobsters were sentenced to four months in jail, but that was far from the end of it.

1986

The labored breathing and sound of phlegm rattling in the throat of the decrepit old man lying beneath the dingy grey sheets played over in my head like an old broken record from the fifties. Sunken cheeks with bulging bloodshot eyes stared into mine. Feeling the rage rise from my guts, I glared back at him with no pity.

"You bastard! You filthy sick bastard! Do you have any idea what you did? The lives you ruined?" I spat the words into his face and reached for his throat.

My head swam and my vision blurred as the stench of urine filled my nostrils. The dirt-filled broken tiles on the nursing home's floor seemed to zoom up to my face without warning. I don't know how long my hands tried to grip his neck before the police arrived. Ice-cold handcuffs clicked onto my wrists and the room spun as echoes of panicked voices rang in my ears.

"Take those cuffs off my sister! Dear God, what's going on here?"

Warm arms held me close as I tried to focus on my sister's face and my vision blurred. Harsh alarm bells blared, then began to fade to the familiar chiming of St. Mary's -- the ever-so-familiar calming bells, gently calling me back to my childhood, the beautiful, beautiful bells of my St. Mary's...

CONTENTS

CHAPTER ONE

St. Mary's, 1945

"Suffer little Children unto me."

-- Matthew 19:14

"Are ya dizzy yet, Billy?" I asked, eyes tearing up as I squinted against the sun.

"Nah. I can stare at that steeple longer than you can."

Our lives -- mine, Billy's, our families', the community -- were centered around St. Mary's Church and school. The schoolyard, where Billy and I stood, both seven years old, trying to outstare each other, was the largest piece of cement anywhere in town. In the summer, we played there and waited for the appearance of the Sisters. They would leave their convent for the summer, returning in August. Their appearance signaled that summer was over and that school would be starting soon.

I shrugged at his dare. "Who cares? This church is more my church than your church anyways. My mom told me my Great-Grandpa DeChant helped build it when he was a little boy. So there!"

"Ahh, Maureen, you're lyin'. You don't even have a dad."

Those were fighting words. "God damn you, Billy Smith!"

I landed one good punch to Billy's freckled pug nose. Next thing, we were rolling over and over, kicking and clawing in the hot summer sun.

I picked up my head in order to get in another good punch, only to see a pair of black, shiny leather high-top shoes. My gaze traveled up ankles covered with thick gray cotton stockings to the hem and folds of a heavy black habit. A huge wooden rosary swung at the waist. Wrinkled hands with crooked fingers hung out of the cuffs, then returned to hide like a turtle to its shell. A black veil framed the ancient prune-face of the school's principal,

Sister Mary Adorika, the oldest, most feared human on the planet.

She held up her crooked index finger, and shook it for what seemed to be an eternity before speaking in her thick German accent. "Vhat are you doing, fighting on Jesus's front lawn?"

Billy and I scampered to our feet and stood frozen to the sidewalk.

"S-s-sorry, Sister," I stuttered.

"And vat is dis I hear, little Maureen, you saying bat vords?" Her twisted bony hand flew out of her black sleeve like a bolt of lightning and struck my mouth with lethal knuckles. With Sister's wrath turned on me, Billy bolted for cover.

"Do you know vat happens to children dat use Got's name in vain?"

My neck throbbed from my head being jolted. The taste of blood filled my mouth, and I couldn't speak.

Her beady steel-blue eyes narrowed. She leaned forward to meet my stare. "Der Devil takes them down to the raging fires of Hell, never to see their mothers again."

She straightened, gave me one last long glare, and shook her head. Her hands disappeared into her sleeves again, and she turned on her heel. My eyes followed her as she returned to her daily ritual of walking and praying while patrolling the schoolyard.

I heard a "Tsk, tsk, tsk," which meant there was no hope for my little lost soul. *I hate her guts so bad, I wish God would send a bolt of lightning and strike her dead,* I thought. *And I hate being a kid, too. Just wait till I grow up. Then people will be nice to me.*

I had no idea how long I stood there. A warm summer breeze rustled the still green leaves of the towering maple trees that lined the church and school grounds. I could feel the sting of salty tears running down my sunburned face and felt so angry with myself for crying.

"Psst, psst. Maureen, over here."

I turned to see Billy poke his head out from behind the maple outside the schoolyard. The gate of the old black wrought-iron fence that protected the sacred grounds of St. Mary's was locked. The pointed tips of the pickets were there to discourage any intruders, but they didn't even slow me down.

I took two steps, jumped to the first crossbar and sprang over the top to freedom, diving behind the tree where Billy waited for me. His sandy blond hair, usually haphazardly parted on the side and plastered down with water, was now completely mussed up from our tussle in the schoolyard, and a rooster tail had very nicely taken shape on the back of his head. He grinned from ear to ear, his small brown eyes dancing. Faded bib overalls and a white undershirt hung on the stick-like body of my one and only friend.

I looked down at his dark-brown high-top shoes, with the hooks at the top for the laces, with envy. I coveted those shoes, but unfortunately for me they were only for boys. I sighed, wishing I were a boy.

We stood toe-to-toe. Billy's sunburned face searched mine, begging for every sordid detail of my heroic encounter.

"I know you're not scared o' her, Maureen. 'Sides, I think she wears big ol' bloomers with a trap door on the back of 'em."

I grinned back through my tears. "Ha Ha, Billy! You say the best stuff. Sorry I punched you. Think she has any hair?"

"Yeah. One time, when she was yelling right in my face, I could see it sticking out on the side of her veil. It was all gray."

Billy pulled his hair on the side of his head until it stood straight out. He leaned forward, nose wrinkled up in disgust, until we were eyeball-to-eyeball, and whispered, "And her breath smells like skunk farts."

We rolled on the ground, clutching our sides with laughter. When we finally caught our breath, we sat, resting our chins on our knees, contemplating our next move. A line of ants trailed up the tree, to where a huge glob of amber-colored sap hung. A mourning dove cooed lazily from a telephone wire overhead. I dug my bare toes into the soft, warm dirt and realized how hungry and thirsty I was.

"Wish I had an orange Popsicle," I said. Then, I sat up straight with a brilliant idea. "Hey, Billy. Wanna take some milk bottles back to John and Jean's so we can split one?"

John and Jean's little corner grocery at the end of our street just happened to have a soda fountain. Taking milk bottles back for the two-cent deposit was the fastest way to get treat money. Swiping them off the neighbors' front porches only added sport to the day's fun. My mouth watered at the mere thought of Popsicles. I wondered if Sister Mary Adorika ever ate one. Come to think of it, I never saw her eat anything. Maybe that was why she was so mean.

"You know my mom don't like me to go to the store by myself," Billy answered, "but sometimes when I go to get my hair cut at Beerchecks Barber Shop, she lets me go across to John and Jean's for some bread or something. I'll go ask, and you go n' find some milk bottles."

Billy lived across the street from St. Mary's and three doors down, while I lived four doors down, but on the same side of the street as the church. We tore down the dirt path for our houses, slowing to a skip until we passed the convent so as not to draw attention from the flock of black-hooded angels within. We crossed Stoney Ridge Road, taking a shortcut across the Wagner's tidy front lawn.

Mrs. Wagner came flying off her front porch in her starched housedress, frantically drying her hands on her apron.

"Billy Smith! How many times have I told you to stay off of my property?" She turned to me and, with a look of utter disgust, eyed me from my mangled hair to my bare feet that hadn't seen soap and water for a week. I almost wished I'd washed them last night instead of sleeping with them stuck in a paper bag to keep the sheets clean.

"Richards, you little mongrel, get off my lawn before you give my family the hoof and mouth disease!" She crossed her arms, glaring down at me. *"Old biddy, old biddy,"* I sang in my head while looking defiantly right in her face.

I waited for the final question she always had to ask every time she saw me. I really wanted to turn and run away from her and go to my Butternut Tree. But running away before an adult was finished talking to you was disrespectful, so I had to just stand there and take what I knew was coming.

She cleared her throat and uttered, just above a whisper: "Tell me, do you ever see your father?"

She made me feel like it was my fault I didn't have a dad. I said, just like I always did, "Nope, he's just as dead as he was the last time you asked me. He got shot in the war."

She sniffed, turned, and walked toward her front door, muttering about my sassy mouth and how it needed to be washed out with soap before I went to Hell for lying.

I hadn't even had lunch yet and was already going to Hell twice today.

The Wagners and the Smiths were archenemies. I never knew what started the feud, but suspect it had something to do with differences of opinion on housekeeping and parenting.

The Wagners' house was immaculate. Each blade of grass stood tall as if charged with guarding the cream-and-brown bungalow. The front lawn of their house was framed by flowerbeds that never saw a weed. A chicken-wire fence divided the yards in a feeble attempt to keep the Smith kids, baseballs, tin cans, and cats off the Wagners' 'estate.'

The Smith family had an empty lot with patches of grass here and there. A round tulip garden -- which just happened to be caught between first and second base -- was obviously losing its struggle to survive.

The Smith's white farmhouse sat on the far side of the lot. The steps missing on the gray front porch guaranteed easy access for their old one-eyed gray cat and her kittens. The family of cats dove under the step just before Billy's foot hit the first board.

"Hey, Ma, kin I go to John and Jean's for an orange Popsicle?" Billy pleaded.

Mrs. Smith stood just inside the screen door in her yellow, daisy-flower print dress, Billy's two little brothers, Jack and Jimmy, clinging to the hem. The three of them were almost knocked over as Billy swung open the door.

Mrs. Smith stepped out onto the porch and looked over at the Wagner house, straightening one of the bobby pins that held her dark-brown hair away from her face. "What have you two been into now? What was Mrs. Wagner yelling about?" Billy flushed and looked down at his shoes.

"I must've stepped on her lawn. I just was excited to see if I could go to John and Jean's for an orange Popsicle," he mumbled.

Her forehead puckered into a frown. "You wait 'til your father gets home. You're getting the strap for sure."

I'd seen the welts on Billy's back from one of those beatings. It made me almost glad my father had left my mom. *Almost, but not really, I think I'd take the beatings any day just to have a dad, no matter how mean he was*, I thought.

"Mrs. Smith," I piped up, "Billy didn't do anything wrong. We just barely touched her crummy ol' grass and she came running out of the house at us. Well, I mean at me. She says I'm a 'mongrel' but she's just a mean ol' rip. My brother Tommy says she puts starch in her drawers and that's why she's so nasty."

Mrs. Smith bit her lip to keep from laughing. "Why, Maureen Richards, what a thing to say. Does your mother even know where you are? Does she ever check on you?" Arms crossed, head tilted up, she looked down her thin nose at me with her usual accusing expression.

Billy shuffled his feet, but knew better than to interrupt his mother. She continued without waiting for my answer. "You'd look so cute in a dress, with your hair in rag curls, instead of those old dungarees you wear every day."

I smoothed my hands down the front of my faded blue blouse, picking at the tiny wrinkled bow in the middle. It was my favorite, because Mother had made it for me. My bare feet were still stained purple from the mulberries that lay on the path in front of the house of the Dunkers, our neighbors.

"Ma, please, kin I go?" Billy begged.

"No, Billy, you need to come in and do your chores."

Billy looked at me sideways and, without another word, slipped past his mom and into the house.

"You go on home now, Maureen. You can call for Billy tomorrow."

Maureen Ann Richards Kostalnick

It was considered rude for a child to knock at the door or ring a doorbell, so you just stood in front of the house and "called" out your friend's name like, "Oh Billy, can you come out and play?"

CHAPTER TWO

Life on Stoney Ridge

"Let he who is without sin cast the first stone."

-- John 8:7

I no sooner got off the porch than the old dull black Ford truck pulled into the driveway. The driver's side door swung open and Billy's dad stepped out in his dingy blue coveralls, waving his hands wildly in the air, a thundercloud of a frown on his face.

"Maureen! You just git on home and stay there."

He came running after me. I tore back across Stoney Ridge and into Mr. Dunker's yard. The mulberry tree was a welcome sight. Once behind it, I peeked out to see Mr. Smith, black lunch box in hand, pull open his screen door and step into his home. My heart was jumping out of my chest. Sometimes Mr. Smith was nice, but most of the time he chased me home when he saw me in their yard.

"Hi dere, kit."

It was Old Man Dunker, sitting on his front porch, smoking a cigarette, drinking his usual can of Pabst Blue Ribbon Beer, and enjoying the sight of the summer sun sinking behind gray clouds that floated lazily against the red- and gold-streaked sky. Mr. Dunker was tall, thin, and rather bent over. His hair was slicked back without a part. Thick rimless glasses sat on his hairy-nostrilled beak-nose.

"Come on up here and talk to ol' Dunka and Kippa," he said.

Mr. Dunker and I got along just fine, seeing as how he was the only person in town who cussed more than I did. But Skipper -- his old, fat, black cocker spaniel -- scared the hell out of me. He would barrel down off the porch, with those bloodshot eyeballs that always had those slimy yellow things in the corners.

"Where's your damn dog?" I yelled.

He slowly picked up his feet off the porch railing, bent over, and caught the obese Skipper by the collar. "It's okay, kit. Kippa's with me."

I edged myself over to the first step and sat on the corner. Dunker reached into the box of chocolates that was always within his reach, and tossed one to Skipper. The dog swallowed it whole and sat and drooled for more.

"Life is tough, kit. You gotta be tough. When I was in the German army, I laid in a Got-damn mut hole for fife years." He took another slug of beer, thin arms hanging out of a starched white undershirt. Skipper put his head on the old man's lap, drooling on the tan trousers tucked into the shiny jet-black army boots he always wore.

I thought about my brother Tommy imitating Old Man Dunker and looked down at my feet to hide my grin. I had not given up on getting my orange Popsicle and was hoping Mr. Dunker was in the usual generous mood he was in when he drank his beer.

He must have read my mind.

"Here, kit," he said, and flipped me a quarter. "Go and get yourself some ice cream."

"Gee, thanks, Dunker." I stood up and started to hightail it for John and Jean's grocery. Skipper flew down the steps after me, spit hanging off his drooping jowls. I jumped up on the running board of Dunker's old Model T, but he still got hold of my dungarees and slimed them as he viciously shook my pant leg.

"Dunker, get your goddamn dog off my leg before he eats my foot off!"

"Here, Kippa, dat's a goot fella."

As the dog turned and ran for Dunker, wiggling its fat body in utter delight, I stepped slowly off the running board and backed up to the worn dirt path. Once Skipper's attention was diverted, I took off running. I sailed past the Kemp's white farmhouse, and Frone Binz's place that had not seen a lick of paint since her ailing brother had died. Frone was sitting under a shade tree, sipping her late afternoon tea.

"You, Richards, come here girl!" Being called by your last name was a sign of disrespect in my town, but I didn't dare ignore her.

Her white hair was pulled back into a bun without a hair out of place. The dark silky dress she wore accented her bony knees. The skirt draped between her skinny legs, which were covered in white cotton stockings. I felt sorry for her, and even liked her a little.

Her oversized orange cat lay curled up in the warm sun. I stooped down to pet it without saying a word. His fur had patches missing from a fight he must have had the night before. I knew just how he felt, and wondered if my lip was swollen from Sister Mary Adorika's cuffing. I could feel Frone's eyes on me, watching my every move.

"You have a really nice cat," I offered.

Her face softened at the mention of her best friend. Her mind wandered a lot. She was always mad about something. She was just not always sure what it was, so she just stayed mad.

She said to me, "Seems I saw you popping the buds on my prize-winning daylilies the other day. Sunday? Yes, I'm sure of it, 'twas Sunday, because Monday was my garden club, so yes, now that I think of it, 'twas Sunday."

Trying to win her approval, I offered an explanation. "Yes, indeed, Miss Binz, you are exactly right, it was Sunday. Only, I was just admiring how beautiful your garden is, when I saw one of those dreadful bugs that eat flowers, and snatched it off for you. Then I ate it. I was really hungry. I bet all the ladies in the garden club wish their flowers looked as good as yours."

She settled back in her rocker, her look of contentment turned to utter confusion. "I heard you were possessed. Did you say you ate a bug?"

I shrugged my shoulders, knowing no matter how hard I tried, she still would not like me. I tore back to the sidewalk along St. Mary's, still hungry and bent on getting my Popsicle.

Old Fritz Balmert was raking up the church grounds in front of the parish house where the pastor, Father Stuber, lived. Poor ol' Fritz had no teeth, and his mouth was so sunken in that his long thin nose almost touched his beard-stubble chin.

I stopped by Fritz and asked, "If it's almost time to ring the bells, can I help?"

The church bells were always rung at exactly twelve noon and six o'clock for the "Angeles." Father Stuber heard my request and strode over to me. He was a tall priest with thin gray hair and huge feet, glasses sitting on the end of a short bulbous nose.

"So you would like to ring St. Mary's bells, young lady? Those ropes you need to pull are heavy, you know. The bells are very large and made from solid bronze." He looked up at the bell tower with pride.

"Good afternoon, Father. They *are* very heavy, but look at my muscles. I'm very strong. Besides, I just jump on the ropes and ride them up and down once Fritz gets them going for me."

It was a contest in the neighborhood as to who got to ring the bells and ride the ropes as high as the knots on the ropes would go.

Father Stuber looked down at me.

"Very well, young lady. If you can recite the 'Angeles' start to finish, you may ring the bells, even though I'm not entirely sure just how lady-like ringing the church bells is." He winked at Fritz as if to say, *"Don't worry, she can't do it."*

Little did they know that if there was one thing I knew how to do, it was pray. Pray my dad would come home and I could be like everyone else. Pray my mom could get out of bed and be happy. But most of all, pray my family would love me, and the neighbors would at least stop chasing me out of their yards.

I puffed up my chest with confidence.

"The angel of the Lord declared unto Mary and she conceived by the Holy Ghost." I bowed my head, squinted my eyes shut as tight as I could, and struck my chest slowly, with reverence, three times, and continued, "Behold the handmaid of the Lord, Hail Mary full of grace, the Lord is with thee, blessed art thou amongst women and blessed is the fruit of thy womb, Jesus. Holy Mary Mother of God, pray for us sinners, now and at the hour of our death. Amen. And be it done unto me according to thy word."

I genuflected and continued, "And the word was made flesh and dwelt among us. Pray for us, oh holy Mother of God, that we may be made worthy of the promise of Christ." I finished and smiled up at Father.

He stared down at me, blinking owlishly. "Exactly how old are you?"

"I'm almost eight, Father, and going into first grade when school starts again."

There was a long pause, and then that look I kept getting from grown-ups. "How is your mother?" he asked gently. "She was in to see me just the other day and seemed so very distraught. It seems she needed money for food for you children. I told her to trust in the Lord and go home and pray. The Lord will provide for those who trust in Him. Are you hungry, child?"

My stomach felt just like someone had punched me really hard. The usual flood of guilt that seemed to take over my whole body left me with an overwhelming feeling of doom. I was sure it was all my fault for being such a bad girl and saying cuss words.

"What's 'distraught' mean, Father? Did my mother cry?"

Father looked down at me and said, "Come with me, child. We'll see if Kathryn has some bread left from lunch."

It took all the courage I could muster to follow him when all I really wanted to do was run home to make sure my mother was okay. However, I followed the priest obediently along the gardens that lined the sidewalk, up to the parish house, and into the modest kitchen.

"Well, well, Father, who do we have here?" Kathryn was so pretty in her pale yellow dress. She walked over to me and knelt down so I could see right into her blue eyes.

The priest answered, "This is Maureen Richards, Laura Richards' youngest. They live in that old house where the dump used to be, about four or five doors down, with the grandparents Ted and Vena DeChant. Such a tragic thing. It was in all the newspapers. I do believe Vena's stroke was due to all the stress put on her by Laura and her children living there. Why, you can only imagine..."

Kathryn continued to hold my hands in hers while looking up at Father Stuber with her mouth open. She cleared her throat before the priest could finish, and looked back at me. "I've just finished baking a cherry pie, dear. Would you like a piece?"

I pulled my hands gently from hers. I was starving but said, "Thank you, Kathryn, but Mother made the best lunch. She's such a good cooker, and I just couldn't eat another bite. I have to go now. Mother will be looking for me."

I turned and ran down the steps of the parish house and found my Lassie under some cool pine trees. I crawled under the prickly branches. I wrapped my arms around my dog's neck, buried my face in her thick golden coat, and cried.

"You never get tired of following me, do you, girl? We don't want a Popsicle anymore, do we? I hate it when people treat me like Mother doesn't take care of me." Lassie snuggled close as I continued to rub her ears and spill my guts.

"She does, and she's the best mother in the whole wide world." I felt the quarter from old man Dunker in my pocket.

"Let's surprise Mother, Donna, and Tommy, and get a Clark bar. Maybe even a Mounds and a Milky Way, 'cause we have a whole quarter. Mother can cut them all up in pieces, and we can share while we listen to our radio programs. I think 'I Love a Mystery' is even on tonight."

My mood brightened as I took off, heels flying, for John and Jean's. Now I had a plan that would fix everything wrong in my life. The houses on this side of the parish house were all the beautiful ones where the rich people lived. Hy Klingshirn was watering his manicured front lawn as I skipped past.

"Hi, Mr. Klingshirn. Your cherry tree looks like it sure has a lot of juicy cherries on it. How do you get so many cherries anyways?"

He turned the hose on Lassie and me, yelling, "You just never mind about my cherries! Me and the missus wait all year for our cherries, and between you kids and the birds, we hardly get any!"

Horses hinder! He looked so funny with that big stomach and those gray pants of his pulled up to his armpits by suspenders. My brother Tommy said if he ever peed in his pants, he'd drown.

Now came the big decision. Do I stay on this side of the street where I might meet up with the Schmidt kids? Joycie and Jacob were the meanest rich kids and always threw big cinders at me.

Or, I could cross Stoney Ridge, but there loomed the Baptist church, a small, stark, whitewood frame structure with a steep shingled roof and a cross at its peak. I didn't know exactly what went on in there, but Catholics were not allowed in.

As usual, Lassie, not sure she was supposed to be following me, wove in and out of the maple trees lining Stoney Ridge. She'd hide behind each one until the coast was clear before darting to the next.

"Come on, girl, we're not scared of Joycie and Jacob."

As I got closer to their house, I could see the two huddled close to the shrubs, squatting down with their heads together, looking at something on the ground. *Good,* I thought, *maybe they won't even see me.* But then my curiosity got the best of me. What were those two sissies up to?

I heard Joycie say, "Give me the matches now, Jacob. You had enough chances to start the fire."

"Shut up," Jacob said. "You got to start the one in the back yard."

Joycie stood up and screamed, "Give me those matches *now*, or I'm telling!" She then turned her plump face right at me. "Jacob, it's her! Let's throw matches at her and catch her on fire!"

They came running toward me in their dark brown orthopedic shoes, Joycie's big pink hair bow flapping as she ran. Jacob's navy blue shorts and knee socks matched her dress. They always looked like they were wearing church clothes and never, ever, got dirty.

"Ugh!" said Joycie. "Look at her. She doesn't even have on shoes, and she dresses like a boy." Joycie held a small box of red-tipped matches in her short fat fingers.

I looked her square in her round bulgy eyeballs, hating her for never giving me a chance. "Never you mind about me, Joycie. I've seen frogs at Bauers's Pond that look like your twin. Can you say 'ribit'?"

Joycie continued her rant as if she hadn't heard a word I said. "Hey, Richards, what are you doing in front of our house? You're not allowed to play with us or even come near us, 'cause our parents say that you run wild and say bad words."

"Give me the matches, Joycie." Jacob grabbed the matches from his sister and started to strike one on the side of the box.

"Quick, Jacob, burn her before she gets away."

My heart was jumping out of my chest at the sight of those two, but I took a slow, deliberate step closer, just daring them to burn me. They stopped in their tracks.

"Take another step and I'll smack you silly," I said.

Jacob towered over me, but my fierceness stopped him. He just stood there, pudgy white legs below neatly pressed shorts.

I continued with my verbal attack. "Why does your mother dress you guys so goofy-lookin' anyways? No wonder you do queer things like try to set people on fire."

Jacob continued lighting matches frantically and throwing them at me, but he was such a big sissy, he never even got close.

"Come on, Lassie, let's get 'em!" Grabbing a handful of rocks, I took aim with my arm coiled while chanting, "Kill, Lassie! Kill!"

They took off, tripping and screaming up their front lawn.

What a couple of chickens those two are, I thought. *Not just chickens, but sissy chickens. That's just what they are.*

Lassie and I went on our way to John and Jean's, and with every step, I tried to understand why they hated me so much. *No matter. I think I'll just beat the livin' crap out of them next time.*

It was starting to cloud up. Thunder rolled in the distance as I opened the screen door to the little corner market. The outside of the building was covered in green shingles, with white awnings covering the tops of the wide windows on either side of the door. John was sweeping up the green cleaning meal strewn across the wood-planked floor. He stopped and leaned on the long-handled broom when I stepped in.

A smile covered his aging face. His bright blue eyes twinkled. "Hey, Jean, look who's here."

Jean was behind the soda fountain, in a perfectly starched blueprint dress, trimmed with white rickrack at the neck and sleeves. She swung her face toward me, smiling beneath her tight gray curls. I climbed up on the light-green marbled seat of one of the six fountain stools to get a better glimpse of the cardboard drums of ice cream.

"Well, fisher girl, have you caught any more bluegills up at Bauers's pond?" asked John.

"Billy and me were fishin' just the other day, and I caught twenty-two bluegills and one bullhead. I hate those bullheads. They have real sharp fins that poke out on each side, so you have to be really careful how you take them off the hook."

John finished sweeping and came over to sit beside me, asking, "What kind of bait do you use?"

"Worms are the best, when you can get them. I found a good spot down by the creek where they hide under the rocks," I explained.

The thunder was getting closer and the sky threatened with mountains of greenish-gray clouds as John looked out the screen door at the sky.

"Sounds like we're in for a storm, fisher girl. Better finish your shopping and head for home." He motioned with his head toward the door.

I jumped off the stool and went straight to the candy counter by the checkout. The brightly wrapped candy bars were all lined up with the penny candies on the top row. Chiclets, Beemans gum, and Ludens and Smith Brothers cough drops sat in a box on the linoleum counter. I grabbed two candy bars -- a Mounds and a Milky Way -- and one big orange jawbreaker for the trip home.

"That'll be eleven cents, fisher girl," Jean smiled across the counter at me.

I reached into my dungarees and pulled out my shiny quarter. Jean hit the key on the front of the cash register and the drawer popped open.

"Better let me put your candy in a sack for you," Jean said. She handed me my purchases with my change, in a little brown bag twisted at the top for safekeeping.

I sailed out the screen door where Lassie waited for me. Big raindrops began falling from the heavy clouds covering the sky. I ran as fast as I could for home, but only got to the front of St. Mary's when the sky opened up.

There is going to be good fishin' after the storm clears, I thought. *The bluegills always bite like crazy after a rain.* The church doors were open, so I darted in, drenched to the skin.

I stood for a minute, dripping, and looked at the beautiful stained-glass windows on either side of the vestibule. The pictures in them were of Jesus in His red robe, holding a white baby lamb. I slowly opened the huge swinging oak doors that led into the back of the dimly lit church. The confessionals were on either side of the doors, with the priests' names on each one. The main aisle was covered with a deep red runner that went all the way up to the altar. The pews were made of thick dark oak that came to a majestic carved peak at the top. The air was thick with the smell of stale incense and flowers.

I stared at the gold tabernacle where the Eucharist was kept behind the little white curtain in front of the small gold doors. *This is almost like mine,* I thought. *My Grampa's father really did buy it, even if Billy doesn't believe me.*

The huge statue of the Blessed Mother holding the Baby Jesus was on the left side of the church, where the ladies sat if they were by themselves and not with their families. To the far right of the altar was the statue of St. Joseph and the gentlemen's side of the church. The pews on either side of the main aisle were for families.

After Gramma had her stroke, Grampa always sat on the St. Joseph side. Mother, Tom, Donna, and I sat on the Blessed Mother's side, because without a dad we were not considered a family. When I went to mass by myself, I sat right in front of the Blessed Mother's statue. I looked up at her beautiful face and said a silent prayer. "Thanks for being my friend, Dear Lady. I always feel better after talking to you. I love you so much."

There was a small figure kneeling in front of the Blessed Mother. I held tightly onto my brown wet sack and crept closer. As my eyes became accustomed to the light, I recognized the wrinkled blue scarf that covered my mother's soft brown curls.

CHAPTER THREE

My Family

"Oh, most holy family, Jesus, Mary, and Joseph, pray for us."

-- Prayers for the Family

Mother's elbows rested on the communion rail, her face buried in her hands. The lit candle cast a golden glow over her small frame. As I stepped closer, I could see her shoulders shaking and hear soft, stifled sobs. My eyes brimming with tears, I gently knelt beside her and wrapped my wet, sun-tanned arms around her.

"It's okay, Mother. I'm here now. Bet I can fix whatever's makin' you cry."

I hugged her, burying my face in her soft cotton dress. She always smelled so good, just like fresh Fels Naptha soap. Her arm wrapped around me in turn, and we knelt there, together. She turned her beautiful face to me and managed a smile. Her face still wet with tears, she sat back on her heels.

"You know, your father should be here with us, Maureen. He loves us all very much. It's just that the war changed him. He never used to drink like that and use terrible language. Never."

Mother looked up at the statue of Mary. Mary's arms were stretched out to us, and she seemed to be looking right into my eyes.

"Do you know what I think, Mother?" My arms were wrapped tight around her still. "I think if we say special prayers every day to the Blessed Mother, and maybe even make her a May altar and bring her fresh violets from my secret violet patch down by the creek, Dad will come home. I'm just sure of it. Let's keep the porch light on every night for him. You'll see. He'll come home, and we'll all come to church and sit right over there where all the families sit together."

I was sharing my own dream, but always had the same sinking feeling it would never happen. Still, I continued. "Won't Mrs. Wagner just be falling out of her seat wondering what's going on. Think I'll just stick my tongue out of my head as far as it'll go at her." I hugged my mother tighter and said, "Let's go home. I have some candy bars for listening to the radio tonight."

We genuflected at the altar and walked hand-in-hand to the back of the church. After dipping our hands into the holy water and blessing ourselves, we quietly left.

The air was damp with the scent of rain and fresh-cut grass. As I walked down the steps of St. Mary's, I looked up at my mother, still clutching her hand. Large dark-brown eyes looked down into mine. A smile started at the corners of her mouth, then spread into a grin.

"So, Maureen, you're going to stick your tongue out as far as you can at poor Mary Wagner?" Mother grabbed her nose to muffle a laugh, as she always did when she knew she should not be laughing but just couldn't help herself.

Mother's mood was changing, and I giggled as I skipped beside her, feeling very proud of myself. The cinders on the path home were wet and stuck to my feet. The condition of my feet did not escape my mother's notice. "By the looks of those feet, you could use a nice hot bath. We have some fresh sweet corn and tomatoes from Grampa's garden for dinner, and I baked some bread this afternoon to fill in the cracks."

Mother doesn't cook when she isn't feeling well, I mused, *so maybe she feels better than I thought.* Hoping to encourage this mood, I said, "You're just the best cooker in the whole wide world, Mother."

As we got close to our long, cindered driveway, Mother and I took the short cut that by now had worn a path across the Dunkers' lawn.

"Evenin' Mrs. Richards." It was Old Man Dunker's wife, Sofie, standing on the porch with her hands on her hips, checking on the aftermath of the afternoon storm. Her hair was mostly gray and neatly tucked into a hair net. She wore a housedress with an apron covered with lavender forget-me-nots. Poor Mrs. Dunker. Not only was she married to Old Man Dunker, but she was so bowlegged that she waddled from side to side when she walked. My brother Tommy said she was either related to a duck or born on a horse.

Mrs. Dunker continued, "That wuz sure some downpour, and the radio wants more. Can I offer you a nice hot cup of coffee, Mrs. Richards?"

Mother scarcely looked up.

"Thank you so much, Mrs. Dunker, maybe another time."

Mother glanced at the lilac trees at the corner of our front porch. Their branches hung heavy with wet, dark, purple blooms. "Oh, just look at those lilacs. The rain seems to freshen everything up so. It's like the whole world could just start up fresh and clean all over again. Why don't you get a mayonnaise jar from under the sink and pick some for Gramma? They're her favorite flower."

"I will, Mother." *Maybe then, Gramma will like me,* I thought.

The old screen door creaked as I opened it. The top hinge was rusted and hung by one bent-over nail. Our home was a garage with a small room that Grampa had added on to the front as a small living room. Then on the far end of the converted 'garage' to what was now the kitchen, Grampa had added one more room. It was a 'porch-like' room with all windows on three sides. Because we needed a place for all five of us to sleep, it became a bedroom for all of us. It was wonderful in the summer, but we froze in the winter, as the room was not heated. Then, when Gramma had a stroke, he built three more rooms on the other side of our house for him and Gramma. The last addition was the front screened-in porch, Grampa's favorite place. He had an old white metal glider he sat on every evening after supper while he puffed on his pipe.

An old flowered couch, with sunken-in cushions, and a matching chair sat at one end of the living room. A floor-model Emerson radio stood between them. I stepped through the kitchen door and looked down at the chipped, gray-painted linoleum.

I thought about my imaginary Indian friend and how impressed he would be at living in a real house, and began showing him around my "teepee" with great pride.

"Look there, Indian, have you ever seen a real table?" A light-green enameled table and chairs sat in the middle of the small room. The tabletop was cluttered with old letters, a misplaced can opener, and some string. I strolled over to the corner of the small room, with my Indian following in awe at the wonder of it all.

"This, Indian, is where we can keep our food cold." I lifted the rusted latch and opened one of the two doors on the front of the icebox. "This is where we put a big block of ice that Max the ice-man brings every Thursday." The dark oak icebox huddled next to the badly chipped cream-colored stove. "And just look here. We can cook on this." I puffed up my chest with pride. My Indian stood with his mouth wide open at the magic of it all. The countertop was faded print linoleum. A small red pump for water was attached to the end of the counter with the spout hanging over the sink.

"Watch this, Indian." I gave the handle a couple of good pumps, and water gushed out in one spurt. "We don't drink this water. We use it to wash our hands and the dishes."

A stainless-steel bucket and ladle, full of drinking water from the well at St. Mary's, sat on the counter.

"Look here. This is clean water we can drink."

An all-too-familiar voice broke my concentration.

"Hey, Maureen, who're you talking to anyways?" Tommy was grinning from ear to ear.

What rotten luck to be found out by Tommy. I had to think fast. "Nobody, you big dummy. I'm practicing my prayers for school."

He looked at me sideways as he stepped out of the door with his usual shit-eating grin on his face. His head popped back in as he thumbed his nose at me and taunted "Got ya last!"

I returned the gesture that meant "kiss my ass" and yelled, "Oh no ya didn't! I got you last, you big dumb Jackass!"

I could hear his voice trail off with the "Got ya last! Got ya last!" chant as I returned to the task at hand.

A small, white-enameled cupboard hung over the sink, its glass doors displaying water-stained shelf paper and chipped cups with mismatched plates. I bent down to examine the shelves under the sink, pulling aside an old flour sack curtain suspended on a line of twine. There, on one of the shelves, sat an empty mayonnaise jar with mouse droppings in it. I called out for my mom.

"Mother, the mouse is back under the sink, 'cause the mayonnaise jar has mouse turds in it."

Mother walked slowly past me, looking nothing like the mom I had just had so much fun with just a few minutes ago. She was all bent over and clutching her stomach. "I'm not feeling very well. I didn't sleep a wink last night. I need to go back to bed. I just can't worry about the mice right now."

What had I done to change her mood? *I guess it must be my cussing,* I thought. But, try as I might, when I got pushed to the brink, the cuss words just flew out of my mouth like shit out of a duck's ass.

I watched her step on the landing that joined our bedroom to the kitchen. On the landing to the left, stairs led down to the basement. The door on the right opened to the outside. Once inside the bedroom, Mother crawled back into the unmade bed and pulled the covers over her head.

"I'm home!" My fourteen-year-old sister, Donna, walked into the kitchen, looked around, and sighed. "Is Mother lying down, Maureen?"

"Yes, and I was just going to pick some lilacs for Gramma." I stood, still holding the mayonnaise jar. Donna smoothed back her long dark-brown hair from her face. I ran up to her. She knelt down so I could throw my arms around her neck.

"You're so beautiful, Donna. Will I ever be as pretty as you?"

"Am I really? I don't think I'm pretty, and you are already beautiful, Boguidie.

"Tell me again why you always call me 'Boguidie'," I said.

"When Mother brought you home from the hospital, she asked me what I thought of you. I was only eight years old, and I said you looked just like a 'Boguidie,' so that's been my special name for you ever since."

"I know who else thinks you're beautiful," I teased her.

Donna blushed as she stood up, smoothing her sleeveless white blouse over her perfectly formed figure.

I continued, "You know Dick and Don Wagner? They always ask me who your boyfriend is. That's usually right after they ask if I ever see my dad."

She rolled her eyes. "Oh, hubba hubba, those two. Tell them it's none of their business. And besides, I'm only fourteen and too young to have a boyfriend. What a couple of 'Oogs.' Look, I got paid today for cleaning the Tomlan's house." Donna reached into the pocket of her side-zipped blue jeans and pulled out five crisp one-dollar bills. "This will make Mother feel better. Let's keep the money in the cupboard, Boguidie." Opening the cupboard door, Donna took out an old, blue-flowered sugar bowl, neatly folded the bills, and put them into the bowl.

She looked around at the kitchen. "You must be hungry. And just look at this place. I'll heat up some water for your bath and wipe up the floor while you soak for a while."

I opened the bathroom door to the usual mound of clothes hanging on a nail behind the door. The unpainted sheetrock was cracked and peeling at the corners.

I looked at myself in the rusted mirror over the sink. *I don't know why my hair gets so tangled,* I thought. *Wish I were a boy. They have short hair and never get tangles.*

The bathroom was kind of a pass-through to Gramma and Grampa's side of the house, with a connecting door opposite the sink. As I looked in the mirror, the door opened, and Grampa stepped in, wearing his old dress pants and a sleeveless, ribbed undershirt.

He observed me in the mirror. "Maureen, hope you're going to comb them hair."

His own neatly combed hair was thinning, but still light brown with a well-placed curl right in the middle of his forehead. He was lean and tanned from years of working the farm, his hands coarse from the unrelenting, backbreaking work. There he stood, all five feet of him, rimless glasses sitting in the hook of his very

French nose. He put his pipe back in his mouth and eyed me critically.

"I'm going to take a bath soon as the water heats, Grampa, and then I'm going to cut some lilacs for Gramma."

His stare softened. "Well, maybe that will cheer her up. That woman has given me no peace all day. Where is yer mother?"

"She had to go lay down. She's not feeling very good again."

Without another word, he pushed past me, yelling for Mother even before he got to her room. I stayed on his heels just in case my mom needed me. "Laura, get up out of that god-forsaken bed and go take care of your mother!"

Mother sat up on the edge of the bed with pure hate glaring in her eyes. She stood and grabbed the first thing her hand touched on the top of the dusty, cluttered dresser. A jar of Noxzema Skin Cream, with the lid screwed on cockeyed, flew past me and smashed all over the floor. Dark-blue pieces of glass glinted, along with hunks of the dried white cream.

Mother screamed, "I hate you! You're not getting away with blaming me any longer! Take care of her yourself, you old bastard!" Mother continued her barrage with jars, a toothless comb, and the handle of a misplaced cast-iron meat grinder.

Grampa danced away from the aerial attack, retreating to his side of the house, cursing his life with his crazy daughter and crippled wife. He took a step back into the kitchen where Donna, Tommy, and I stood wondering what the hell had just happened.

He motioned toward us with his pipe, making his usual comment regarding Mother's all-too-frequent hysterical blowups: "You kids are the ones I feel sorry for. You are the ones that will have to deal with all of this someday."

His words played back in my mind. *"Someday?" Today's bad enough.*

In painful silence, Tommy and I helped Donna clean up the glass and trash from every corner of the tiny kitchen. Mother returned to her bed like nothing had happened. Tommy was the first to break the silence.

"Teddy was smart to lie about his age and join the service to get out of this place."

His words sent a panic through me. *Who's going to leave next*? I wondered. *I don't even remember Teddy living with us.*

Donna must have recognized the look on my face. She knew I was getting ready to bolt out the door to my Butternut Tree. In her typical "business-as-usual" manner, she said, "You still need a bath, Boguidie. The water's hot on the stove, so go get in the tub. The warm water will make you feel better."

I scampered to the bathroom, dismissing the haunting thought that things could get worse.

Donna grabbed the pot of steaming water and approached, warning, "Stand back, Boguidie. This is really hot." She poured the water in the tub and put in her hand to test the temperature. "Ahh, this is just right. Get in."

The water was not more than an inch deep. But, as usual, she was right.

I shucked my clothes with a sigh. "Wish I could have nice hot water all the way up to the top of the tub, the way the movie stars do."

Donna grinned. "Well, here's a bar of Sweetheart Soap, 'Sheena, Queen of The Jungle.' You'll just have to pretend the tub is full." I just about lived at the creek at the end of Grampa's property, and thus truly was 'Sheena, Queen of the Jungle,' who roamed the wild with my secret imaginary Indian friend.

Donna laughed and I got into the tub. The water felt deliciously warm. I proceeded to lather up with the fragrant pink soap and sing, as loud as I could. I sang the nastiest song I had ever learned from my drunken father, feeling better by the moment.

"Oooh...fire in the mountain, snakes in the grass. The old man died with a cork up his ass. The wind blew in and the wind blew out, and made the old man live again.

Oh, the bear went over the mountain, the bear went over the mountain, the bear went over the mountain to see what he could see. He fell in a hell of a dark hole. Sparks flew out of his asshole the night before the war."

The door flew open and in came Donna.

"That's not a very nice song, and I told you before, young ladies don't use bad words. Now, you have to promise to stop saying bad words."

"I don't know what makes my mouth say 'em. They just keep coming out when I least expect it."

"I know you hear Dad swear when he comes around, but that's him, not us. We're young ladies, and we don't talk like that." She knelt beside the tub and started washing my arms and back, saying, "Supper's on the table for you and Tommy. Mother's still not feeling so good, and I have to run down to John and Jean's to call Dr. Smith to come and see her. I want you and Tommy to eat something, and please, don't fight."

Owning a telephone was a luxury we didn't enjoy where we lived, at 2788 Stoney Ridge Road. The corner grocery store was a better choice for making a call than bothering a neighbor.

"I'm not hungry," I said. "I want to come with you."

"I need you to be grown up now and stay with Tommy." She looked like she was going to cry, but she didn't. She never did.

"Sure, I think I'm almost grown up anyways. If Tommy pulls out his ears at me, and sticks out his tongue, I won't even care. He's twelve years old and should know better than to do that to me. I think he just likes to hear me cuss. That's what I think."

"Wrap up in this towel, and I'll try to get a comb through this hair."

"Ow! Stop! You're pulling all my hair out, and I'm going to be bald and have to wear a bonnet like Nancy Pinkersgill!"

Nancy was really bald and somewhat slow, but I liked her just fine. I just didn't want to be bald and have to wear a silly-looking bonnet. *That's' all I'd need,* I thought, *one more thing to be teased about.*

"It's okay Boguidie, there's just one more rat I need to get out. Here's some clean underwear."

"Oh good, these are my new underwear that came from the Sears Catalog. Mom ordered them for me." Smoothing back my hair, I pulled on my white Sears and Roebuck undershirt. After finding the front from the back, I gingerly stepped into my new underpants that Mother had ordered two sizes too large so I would get more wear out of them. The only problem was that they came up to my "chesters" so they would fit. I grabbed a wrinkled but fresh pair of overalls from the laundry and jumped into them.

Feeling like a queen in all her glory, I made my grand entrance into the kitchen. Tommy was sitting at the table holding a huge piece of Mother's fresh baked bread covered in butter and applesauce. Donna had set the table for us, and came and sat between Tommy and I to say Grace. We folded our hands and bowed our heads.

"Bless us, Oh Lord, for these thy gifts which we are about to receive, through thy bounty through Christ our Lord. Amen."

Tommy took a huge bite of his bread, looked at me, and crossed his eyes while he chewed.

"Your face is going to stay like that with one eye looking at the other, Tommy." I sat munching on my sweet corn, feet swinging, feeling very self-righteous and in control of the whole situation. After all, I'd just lived through a skirmish that would make one of Old Man Dunker's war stories look like a walk in the park.

Donna said, "Tommy, stop that. I asked you to be more grown up tonight. I need your help, okay?"

"Yeah, okay. I'll wait till Mother's feeling better. Then I'll torture Gravel Girdie here."

He knew where my goat was tied. I hated the name of that ugly, wild-haired lady in the comic strip, even if I didn't comb my hair. He glared at me like he hated me. But I did have my ace in the hole.

"I've got some candy bars to eat while we listen to 'I Love A Mystery' and 'The Shadow,' you horse's ass. So if you want some, quit being so nasty." I flew off my chair and grabbed my sack of candy and swung it in front of his nose. "You can even cut up the candy bars and eat the bigger pieces, because you're bigger and dumber. How's that, Eagle Beak?"

Donna stood still with her mouth clamped shut, trying with all her might to conceal her grin. Finally, after regaining her composure, she cleared her throat. "That sounded better until you got to the horse's ass, dumber, and Eagle Beak part. How are we ever going to get you to clean up your mouth?"

I looked at her and wished I were a different kind of a sister to Donna and Tommy. But as hard as I tried to stop swearing, when I got mad I cussed like a sailor.

Donna left, and Tommy and I finished our supper. Tommy's mood changed when one of his favorite pastimes came to mind.

"Hey, Maureen, let's surprise Mother and Donna and clean up the kitchen. We could even redecorate and move the table and chairs and stuff."

We sprang into action. I scraped off the plates into Lassie's bowl, and pumped some water into the dishpan. We cleared off the kitchen table and stuffed everything into the sink.

"Let's move the table under the window, so we can see outside when we're eating."

Of course, the real challenge was to peer through the seasons of dirt that coated the glass and barely let the light in.

"You have the best ideas, Tommy."

We had just finished when Donna came back.

"This looks really nice. And I like the table under the window much better. Dr. Smith is coming right over. Did you check on Mother"?

"She's just been sleeping," I said. "So we didn't know if we should tell her dinner was ready or not, so we just waited till you came back."

There was a knock at the front door, and I could see Dr. Smith through the screen. He was tall and very handsome. His white starched shirt was open at the neck, with the sleeves rolled up. He walked into the kitchen carrying his black bag.

"The bedroom's this way, doctor," said Donna, leading him into our shared bedroom, where Mother was sleeping.

"It's okay, kids. You can wait in the kitchen while I check your mom."

We left the door cracked open and sat on the floor to listen.

"Well hi, Mrs. Richards. It's Dr. Smith. How are you feeling?"

"I'm just so tired all the time, and have so much pain in my abdomen. It's that time of the month again and, well, I seem to be bleeding most of the time."

"I just want to listen to your chest and take your blood pressure. Have you been taking the vitamins I prescribed for you?"

"Not yet. I've been waiting to get a few dollars from my husband. He's been looking for work in Cleveland, with the depression and all. He stays at his mother's, you know, and comes home whenever he can." This was the story Mother told, but somehow everyone knew they were divorced.

"How did your ribs get so bruised? And what are these fingerprints doing on the sides of your arms?"

"I must have bumped into something. I'm such a klutz."

Dr. Smith took off his stethoscope, and took Mother's hand in his.

"I don't believe you bumped into anything. And what's more, I don't think you are a klutz, either. I'm your Doctor. You can talk to me in strict confidence. I'm here to help you however I can."

Mother put her face in her hands and started to cry. "Oh, what must you think of me? I'm truly sorry. It's just that things have not been going so good, and Chuck tries so hard. He really does, really."

"We talked last month about having a hysterectomy, and I'm afraid things have only gotten worse. We have no choice now, Laura. I'll make arrangements at the hospital to have this done as soon as possible. You're just losing too much blood."

"Maybe if I just stay off my feet for a few days, I'll get better."

"We tried that last time, dear. I'll stop by tomorrow afternoon and tell you what day you're going in. I promise to take very good care of you, and you'll feel so much better after the surgery."

Dr. Smith stood up, and we crept back from the door and sat at the kitchen table.

"I have a feeling that somehow you heard every word your mom and I said." Dr. Smith stood at the table and smiled down at us.

"Just how sick is our mother?" Donna's face was white, and her lips started to quiver.

The doctor pulled out a chair and sat down.

"Your mother is going to be just fine, but she needs to have an operation. I'm sure you kids will be a big help to her and do everything you can around the house. I told your mother I'd make arrangements at St. Joseph's Hospital and stop by tomorrow to talk to her. Is there any way I can get a hold of your dad? Do you have a phone number where he can be reached?"

"No, we don't. He just shows up every now and again, and we never know when he's coming home." Donna continued to look down at her shoes as she talked.

"Dr. Smith, I was just going to take these flowers to Gramma. Do you want to come and see her, too?" I asked.

"That's a real good idea, young lady."

I took his hand and led him out onto the front porch and over to Gramma's front door.

"Grampa, it's me, and I have Dr. Smith with me. Mother has to have an operation, and me and Donna and Tommy are going to take care of her. Can we come in?"

Grampa opened the screen door.

"Hi there, Doc. Won't you come in? It's good to see you. How's the missus?"

We stepped into the living room. The hardwood floor had an area rug in the middle with an overstuffed love seat and couch bordering it edges. A cherry wood coffee table with Queen Anne's legs sat in the middle. The dark oak china cabinet was filled with pink-and-cream dishes. The tall Boston Cooler glasses, with frosted ponies on a carousel, sat neatly on the top shelf. Classical music was playing softly on the Victrola.

Gramma sat in her wheelchair, her soft white hair pulled up in a neat bun. With her crippled right arm drawn up to her chest, she held out her left hand to the doctor.

"Those bright blue eyes of yours have an extra twinkle today, Vena. Just what kind of trouble have you been getting into?"

Gramma took his hand, squeezed it, and laughed. "You are a wascal now, aren't you."

Gramma had a hard time saying her "R's" ever since her stroke.

"Rascal, rascal," she laughed. "Oh for God sakes a life, I can't even talk stwaight any more. Straight, straight," she corrected herself.

Dr. Smith smiled comfortingly.

"What have I been up to? Well, I've been asking Ted to take down that wall there that separates our living room from Laura's. That man, that man, he just doesn't listen, so I took a hammer to it myself, as you can see." She sat back in her wheelchair and gave a final nod of approval to herself.

A gaping hole in the middle of the wall, with plaster all over the floor under it, was proof enough of her determination.

"Just listen to me going on. What's this about my Laura now?" She leaned forward in her chair, smoothed her blue print dress over her knees, and held her paralyzed fist with her good hand.

"Laura needs to have an operation, a hysterectomy to be exact. I'm hopeful this will also help her mental condition. I know how painful this subject must be for both of you, but what can you tell me about her husband? I've noticed some suspicious marks on her arms. If there is any abuse going on, I need to report it to the proper authorities."

I sat unnoticed on the couch, and somehow knew this was not the time to ask any questions. After all, children were to be seen and not heard. Gramma took her flowered hankie from her pocket and dabbed at the corners of her eyes. Grampa took his pipe from his mouth and leaned forward with both elbows on his knees.

"I don't know how much more I can take. She's brought on all her own problems." He puffed on his pipe before continuing. "I've got Vena here, and God knows her stroke came from having just too much with Laura and them kids."

Grampa's face was getting redder by the minute, and his voice louder. Things were going from bad to worse, and I could write the next scene by heart on how Mother was just a "millstone" around his neck. I slipped off the couch, out the door, and straight down the path to my creek and my tree.

The warm breeze on my face seemed to bring me peace with every step I took. My feet were clumped with mud, and pant legs soaking wet from the tall grass I ran through. As I sat on a rock at the waters' edge under my Butternut Tree, I was finally able to cry. Snorting and licking tears from the corners of my mouth, I tried to sort out everything.

"Just wait till I grow up, tree. There's not going to be any yelling in my house." I wrapped my arms, as far as they could reach, around the old Butternut. The coarse bark was still warm from the afternoon sun. The breeze caught the huge branches at the top of the tree, and gently rocked me as I held tight to the trunk. A robin sang her good-night song in the distance, quieting my fears. I looked up through the trees, to the Blessed Mother's beautiful blue sky.

"Dear Lady, this is your friend, Maureen, at the Butternut again. Please help me grow up really fast, so I can help my mother feel better. And please bring my dad back, so we can be a real family. I just want to be like everyone else. Besides, I think I have too much that hurts inside, and I am just a kid. I know I should not say this, but I think they are all fucking nuts. Sorry. I'll even stop saying bad words if you just fix this. I promise. Thanks an awful lot. I love you, Blessed Mother."

I rolled up my sopping cuffs and stuck my muddy feet in the creek. The water was warm, and I wriggled my toes at the little tadpoles as they darted around the bottom. I washed my feet and wiped them off on a clump of grass. Pant cuffs still rolled up to just below my knees, I walked slowly back up the path, past the old chicken coop. There was Grampa's spade, still stuck in the mud right where I had left it. I pulled it out of the ground, hoisted it over my shoulder, and headed for the basement. I arrived at the outside entrance of our basement and opened the heavy door Grampa had constructed from leftover two-by-fours and barn wood.

I stepped inside, and the door creaked shut behind me. I carefully placed the shovel in the corner with the rest of Grampa's tools. The light from the small glass-paned door at the top of the stairs shed just enough light for me to see the coal furnace on one side and the old wringer washer with concrete wash tubs on the other. My dog Lassie had followed me into the basement and stretched out on the cool cement floor. I grabbed a rag and started wiping off her wet fur. The stick-tights were stuck on all over her legs and tail.

"Boy, you sure are a mess, girl. I'll try to get some of these out." I sat and started to gently pull the weeds from her thick coat.

"Say there, little Maureen, what are you and Lassie up to now?" Grampa stepped out of the fruit cellar with a tin cup of his homemade apple cider. He walked over to where Lassie and I were sitting and stooped down slowly. My eyes searched his face, as it was not often I saw him up this close. His face was solemn. He pushed the old felt dress hat that he wore to work the farm in to the back of his head.

"Some things are hard to understand, little Maureen. I just want you to know you'll always have a home here, no matter what."

"What was Dr. Smith talking about my mother for? What happened to her?"

"You'll understand when you're a grown-up. Right now, all you need to understand is your mother needs an operation, and we're all goin' t' pitch in and help, to make sure you kids are all right and Laura gets on her feet again." He knelt down on one knee when he saw me run with open arms stretched out to him.

I wrapped my arms around his neck and hugged him. I swallowed hard, practicing the vow I made to myself never to cry again.

"Thanks, Grampa. You're the best Grampa ever."

He stood up and shuffled out the door. I watched him as he stood at the back of the yard, looking out over his vegetable garden, the smoke from his pipe drifting with the breeze. All five feet of him stood very tall. The sun was starting to set, the sky streaked with red, yellow, and gold. The katydids and tree frogs started their nightly ritual of song. I ran up the basement steps and into the kitchen.

Mother stood leaning on the kitchen sink, washing some dishes, in her worn pink chenille robe.

"Hi, Mother. Is it time for our radio programs yet?"

"Tommy, turn on the radio to 'Hermits Cave.' It's really getting good," she said. "Let's make some popcorn, Maureen. Would you like that?"

"Yeah, and I have candy bars, too. We can have a feast."

The radio blared the eerie music to "Hermits Cave" from the small living room, and we all gathered around for the evening's entertainment. The rich, buttery smell of popcorn filled the tiny house. Mother sat curled up in the old flowered chair. Tommy was next to the radio so as not to miss a single word, and Donna and I cozied up together on the couch.

"Why don't we just cut off these stupid springs that keep poking me in the butt, Donna?" I asked.

"Here, sit on this pillow and don't talk anymore, runt." Tommy tossed an old satin pillow at me, which I put on top of the protruding spring.

We hung on every word of "Hermits Cave" and "I Love A Mystery," and devoured the popcorn and candy bars Mother had cut in pieces -- as eating a whole candy bar was considered rude and piggish.

I had my paper and pencil ready for the address to send for my own special secret decoder ring, and Donna copied it down for me. Tommy had disappeared from his chair -- we thought to use the restroom. Seconds later, though, he appeared all dressed up in one of Gramma's old maroon-flowered dresses and a big floppy hat with a huge daisy on the top. His skinny legs were covered in cream-colored cotton stockings that were rolled down to his ankles. Mother doubled up in laughter.

"Oh my God, Tommy! Who are you tonight?" she managed to choke out. He had a very large alligator purse, and proceeded to stick his whole head in it while digging through it with one hand.

"I'm Gallstones, and I can't seem to find my church envelope. I'm afraid if I can't find it, Father Stuber will kick my bony ass out of church. And we all know his feet are big enough to do it, too." He said this in a raspy voice that we all recognized as Mrs. Buldoff's, whom he had dubbed "Gallstones." We all howled until our stomachs hurt. It was so good to see Mother laugh. Tommy's imitation, as usual, was perfect.

"You kids clean up. I need to get some sleep tonight."

Mother went to bed and I headed for the front porch. I could hear the old glider squeaking back and forth, and knew Grampa was having his after-dinner pipe. I was not disappointed. As I opened the screen door, I could see the reflection of the streetlight off of his glasses. I walked out into the cool night air and sat across from him in an old metal chair.

"Tell me again what it was like when you were a boy, Grampa." I could hear his lips puffing on his pipe, and this meant he was getting a story together, as he loved talking about the old days as much as I loved hearing about them. He continued peeling his apple with his jack knife.

"Well, ya know, when I was a youngster and lived up on the farm, those winters got mighty cold. There were fourteen of us altogether, and we boys -- all five of us -- were a rowdy bunch. So my mother, God rest her soul, put us all up in the attic to sleep." Grampa puffed his pipe and started to chuckle.

"That attic, it so happened, was so cold, Mother stored all the winter vegetables and fruit up there like apples, potatoes, and turnips. Well, the thing of it was, once in bed, you didn't dare poke your head up, lest you get hit in the head with a flying turnip." He paused and puffed on his pipe and chuckled to himself.

"I can't begin to tell you how many times I bounced turnips off of poor Justin's head, and you know he never was quite right. Can't help but feel a little guilty there." He broke into a full laugh and had to wipe his nose with his handkerchief. I moved over to the glider and sat with Grampa, listening to him puff on his pipe and watch the lightning bugs fly upward, light up, and sink down, in an almost musical pattern.

"That's a good story, Grampa. Got any more?"

He pulled out his pocket watch to check the time. "Well, ya see, on the farm, we had chickens, and Mother sent me and Justin out to catch one for dinner." He pulled his pipe out of his mouth and shook his head in laughter. "That was easier said than done. We chased that gull-darn chicken every which way until Justin took a dive and finally caught it. It flapped and squawked as he held it upside down by its feet. I pulled the old hatchet out of the block, and Justin held the chicken's head. You ever see a chicken get his head chopped off?"

I took a breath to cover my disgust. "Oh sure, Grampa. Billy's dad does it all the time, and the thing runs all over the barnyard with no head. We just don't think about it when we're eating Sunday chicken dinner, right Grampa?"

"Don't you worry about that, little Maureen. The good Lord gave us chickens to eat. It's been a long day for all of us. I think we'd best get some sleep. I have a lot of work to do bright and early tomorrow. Moving that huge pile of rocks down by the creek has got to be done. If that water keeps eating away at the soil, there'll be nothing left in years to come of the old homestead. I'm doing this for you kids. You kids will always have something here with this place. Always. Only problem is, that darn George -- most worthless farmhand a man ever could have -- never shows up for work."

He puffed on his pipe and walked into the house, chuckling at his joke. He did a quick little shuffle dance before disappearing through the door. Everyone knew George was Grampa's imaginary farmhand, who got blamed for every mishap on the small farm.

The house was quiet. I turned on the porch light for my dad, for the first time of many times to come, hoping and praying he'd come home to stay. I quietly slid under the covers and snuggled up to my mother.

Donna and Tommy were in their beds at the far end of the room. This particular room was intended to be a back porch, so it was glassed in with windows on three sides. It was wonderful in the summer, but we froze in the winter, as the pipe that carried the heat from the coal furnace always fell off the one and only vent to the room.

The crickets sang their lullaby, and the soft breeze rustled the leaves of the old maple tree just outside the window. The tree was actually growing into the side of the house, but cutting a tree was a sin to Grampa, so it was left to grow.

"Who knows what evil lurks in the heart of man? The Shadow knows," came a deep voice from Tommy's bed, and a direct quote from the radio program, "The Shadow," which we had just finished listening to.

Donna was the first to react. "That's it. I'm asking for a transfer to another dormitory in the morning."

"Yeah, well, with your luck, dear sister, they will think you said 'lavatory' and you'll end up in Old Man Dunker's bathroom. And you can only imagine what that smells like, with his diet of sauerkraut and beer."

We were out of control, and Mother finally said, "Okay, okay, that's all very funny, but now I need to go to sleep, or else."

"Else what, Ma? Are ya gunna break off my arm and beat me with the bloody stump?"

"Oh, Tommy, you know how I hate that saying. Your Irish grandmother used that term, and it's so crude. Now go to sleep, and I don't mean maybe."

It got quiet for a minute or two, then a pillow-stifled snort would break the silence and we'd start up all over again. I snuggled up to my mother, rubbed my toes together, and drifted off to sleep with big plans for Billy and me in the morning.

Maureen Ann Richards Kostalnick

CHAPTER FOUR

Bauers's Pond

"Angel of God, my guardian dear, to whom his love commits you here. Ever this day be at my side, to light, to guard, to rule, to guide..."

-- Given to M.A.R.K by Sister Mary Daniel

Old Henry, our rooster, perched on the fence and greeted the day. The Jenny Wren in the Lilac started her song, first softly, and then louder as the robins and sparrows chimed in.

This was one of the best parts of the day, just cozying up next to my mother, inhaling the cool fresh breeze that gently blew across our bed, and listening to the world I loved wake up. This was the part of my life that I knew I could count on never changing. I fell back to sleep with comforting thoughts of everything being right in my world. God had truly blessed me with the ability to put the horrid happenings of the previous day behind me and just start over like they had never happened.

"Laura, Tommy, Donna!" Grampa stood on the landing, just outside our bedroom. "It's almost eight o'clock, and Henry's been off his perch for hours. Time to get up." The smell of fresh coffee and Grampa's potato pancakes drifted in from his kitchen. "Gramma's wanting someone to jelly her toast, and I made extra pancakes. Better get them before that no-account 'George' sinks his teeth into 'em!"

He shuffled out the door in his bib overalls, flannel shirt, and, as always, his felt dress hat. I watched him as he passed our window, dipping into his chewing tobacco and stuffing a chunk into his cheek.

I crawled out of bed and jumped into my dungarees that laid in a clump at the foot of the bed, then ran in to see Gramma. I stopped to look in the mirror to see what she would find wrong so I could fix it. Sure enough, there was dirt on my face --

probably remnants of my trip to the creek the day before. A quick swipe of the washcloth that sat in a crumbled ball in the sink did the trick.

Gramma was sitting in her wheelchair in front of the tiny kitchen table. Her soft-boiled egg sat in an egg-cup, the top of the egg cracked neatly off. She looked up as I stepped into her kitchen.

"Need some help with your toast, Gramma?"

She reached for her crippled arm with her good hand and held it. Tears rolled down her wrinkled face.

"Yes, yes, I can't even put jelly on my toast. I wish to God I were dead."

I picked up the silver butter knife and scooped out some strawberry jelly. I could still remember how, before her stroke, everything had been perfect in her house. Linen tablecloths and fine china were on her table every day. Then Gramma had dressed just like she kept house, meticulously, in navy-blue suits with her hair pulled neatly up in a bun. On Sunday afternoons, all the fine ladies and gents would come over to play Bridge after a roast beef dinner with all the trimmings. I was littler and cuter then, and probably had not learned to curse yet. Thus, I was accepted and got an occasional pat on the head.

I went to work on Gramma's toast, knowing exactly how she liked it, feeling grateful for the opportunity to win her approval, no matter how slight. The jelly had to cover every corner of the toast, including the crust. I then cut the bread diagonally.

"That's it. That's exactly wight." She shook her head and corrected herself as she always did. "Right, right. For God-sakes-a-life, will you just listen to the way I sound?"

"You sound a lot better than the Muller kids do, Gramma. Sister always yells at them. She says they're just too lazy to pronounce their words right. Plus, they really smell terrible. You don't stink, Gramma, not even one tiny little bit."

She had just dunked her toast into her coffee and was ready to take a bite, but rested her hand on the table instead. Her shoulders moved up and down slightly as she enjoyed a well-deserved laugh. Then she said, "Can you get the milk from the porch? I heard Dairymen's truck earlier, and it will sour if it's left out too long."

I carried in the glass quart bottle of milk, intrigued by the heavy cream that floated to the top of the bottle.

"Gramma, would you like some of this cream for your coffee? Or should I shake it up for you?"

"Just a little cream for my coffee will do just fine. I have something I want you to do for me today. That darn, dirty old hat your Grampa wears is just a fright! Bring me my purse. It's there in the closet."

I opened the door to the cedar-lined closet, took out Gramma's black leather purse, and gave it to her. She pulled out her worn coin purse and took out a shiny quarter.

"This is yours if you swipe that darn, dirty old hat and just throw it in the creek. It can be our secret." She pressed the quarter into my hand and folded my fingers around the coin.

"But Gramma, Grampa hardly ever takes it off. I just don't think I can do it. But I'll try, just for you."

I knew Grampa always left his hat on the back railing when he came up from the creek to wash up and have his noon meal. I was also smart enough to know I'd be the first one he'd come after if his hat disappeared...again, as this was not Gramma's first attempt to get rid of "that darn, dirty old thing' of a hat."

She leaned back in her chair. So far, so good, but I knew she was not finished with me yet.

"If I hear you saying one more bad word, I'm going to tell the Sister at school and she'll tell all of the kids what a bad girl you are."

She must think I'm really dumb, I reasoned. *She can't even butter her toast.*

How the hell is she going to get over to school to tell the sisters?

Just then, the screen door opened.

"Good morning, Mrs. DeChant. The Laubs's Bakery truck is here and at your service. Do you need any bread or baked goods?" John, the bakery delivery truck driver, stepped in with his silver tray of cinnamon raspberry and pineapple strudels.

"Oh, Johnny, did you ever time this just 'w-right'. Come over here and let's have a look at what you have today."

He came into the kitchen in his light-blue shirt with "Laubs" written in red lettering over his pocket. The pastries were wrapped in cellophane, but the delicious aroma still filled the kitchen.

"I'll have the raspberry with nuts."

He searched the tray. "I think I have one with nuts in the truck." He looked at me and added, "Come out to the truck and save me a trip back up the drive, girlie."

I just stood there looking at him. He was one of those grown-ups that always knew all the right things to say in front of other grown-ups, but was really kind of creepy.

"The cat got your tongue? Okay I'll sweeten the deal and throw in a free donut."

I could feel Gramma's disapproving glare on the back of my head, so I answered. "Sure, that will be good. I love donuts."

He walked out the door in front of me, and I caught it just before it slammed against my head. I followed him dutifully down the long, cindered driveway to the cream-colored delivery truck with the name "Laubs" in big red lettering on the side. I stood with my head leaning past the folding glass door, looking at the stacks of silver trays full of bakery goods that lined either side of the truck.

John finally came to the door, holding Gramma's pastry in one hand and my donut in the other. As I looked up at him, he held the pastries directly in front of his belt for me to take. I took them from his hands

-- only to see his *thing* sticking out of his unzipped pants.

What felt like the electric shock I got from touching Urigs's cow fence raced through my body and landed in the pit of my stomach. John was grinning from ear to ear, and said, "I would not tell anyone about this, if I were you. I know all about you. And who would believe you, anyway?"

I turned and walked back up the long driveway without saying a word -- then or ever. Inside, I sat Gramma's pastries on her table. Then I tore out the door for Billy's house before anything else could happen.

The air was still cool and fresh, and the locusts sang lazily in the morning sun. I tore across Stoney Ridge and ran around to the back porch to call for him. The old mother cat was lying in the sun, nursing her kittens. I picked up my favorite orange one and held it to my chest. Its belly was huge, and the tiniest little pink tongue protruded from its mouth. The kitten continued the suckling motions of nursing.

I kissed its head and gently placed it back with its mother.

A tire swing, hanging from an old pear tree, showed all the wear and tear of four boys swinging from it. A large groove was gouged out of the dirt, directly beneath. I climbed to the top of the tire and straddled the thick, frayed rope knotted around it. I sang out, "Oh, Billy, can you come out and play?"

The screen door banged open, and Billy stepped out with his fishin' pole made from a crooked maple branch. The black fishline was wound in a ball at its tip with the fishhook, sharp end first, in the middle of the ball. A red-and-white bobber was clipped halfway down the line.

Billy knelt down in front of an old rusty can filled with damp dirt. "Just look at these beauties." He dumped the can out on the porch and a pile of night crawlers fell out. "Me and my dad caught 'em last night with a flashlight. Boy, you gotta grab 'em quick before they go back into their holes. Go 'n get your pole and meet me at Bauers's Pond by the overflow."

Bauers's Pond, directly across from my house, was the best fishing hole around. I retrieved my pole from the basement and tore for the pond and Billy. Red-winged blackbirds chattered noisily as they hung on the cattails. An old log floated at the overflow with a painted turtle sunning itself on it. Billy sat in our favorite spot, baiting his hook with one of his prized night crawlers.

"Over here, Maureen." Billy talked just above a whisper so as not to scare the fish. A snake skimmed across the water and disappeared under the log.

"Can I borrow a worm, Billy?" I whispered back.

He reached in the can and pulled out a long one. He pinched it in half and gave it to me, saying, "This'll be plenty." He tossed his line in and sat staring at the bobber, clutching the pole, ready to spring into action if the bobber went down.

I put my line in the water, far enough from Billy's to keep the two lines from getting tangled, and said, "Watch my pole. I really want to catch that turtle. Look! There's babies on the log with her."

I slowly crept through the weeds to the water's edge, opposite the log. Those babies were so cute, I had to have one at all costs. I carefully waded into the water, clothes and all, not taking my eyes from the turtles for a second. Up to my waist in the muddy water, I waited until just the exact right moment to make my move. I lunged. The turtles dove into the water.

"Damn it, I almost had 'em!" I crawled out of the water, sopping wet, and went back to sit with Billy.

Billy stood up. "Look at your leg, Maureen. It's bleeding. Don't move." He leaned over and pulled a big old black bloodsucker off my calf. "Wow, he's a dandy. Does it hurt?"

"Nope, not really. I didn't even feel the thing on me. Thanks, Billy."

My bobber went down, and I jerked my pole out with a blue gill on the end of it. "Wanna have a contest to see who gets the most fish today?"

"Yeah, but that one doesn't count. We have to start even." Billy paused, and leaned over to me, all the time just looking at his fishin' pole. "Did you hear somethin' comin' from the cattails behind us?" he whispered.

I turned to him slowly, sneaking a peek behind us. "It's Joycie and Jacob. They think they are spying on us. I'd recognize that big ugly bow anywhere."

Without even looking at them, Billy hollered, "Look out for the snake!"

They came screaming out of the brush.

Once again, Billy and I were clutching our sides, laughing at the sight of those two sissies holding onto each other and jumping up and down and screaming. After we'd laughed our fill, Billy picked up his fishin' pole, saying, "Are ya comin', Maureen? The fish will never bite now, thanks to those two." He disappeared into the weeds and all I could see was the top of his pole, heading for home.

Joycie and Jacob had made their way out of the cattails and peered out of the tall grass at the top of the steep hill above the water's edge. They were frantically grabbing dirt clumps to throw at me. Just when I thought they couldn't get any dumber, they did.

"Get her, Jacob!" In Joycie's wild frenzy to stone me to death, she took one step too many and came flying down the hill, bow and all, right into the pond.

Her bow could float, but she didn't.

"I'll save you, Joycie!" Jacob and his orthopedic shoes jumped in after her.

He didn't float either.

The thought crossed my mind to just roll up my fishin' pole and head for Billy's house, but I didn't. The two of them were thrashing in the water something fierce. First, Jacob climbed to the top of Joycie's head for air. Then she grabbed at him, pulling him down.

As much as I was enjoying this whole show -- and no one deserved to drown more than those two -- I waded in to my waist and extended my pole to them. They grabbed hold, and crawled up on the bank, coughing, sputtering, and crying, all at the same time. I couldn't help but feel sorry for them.

"It's okay. You're all right now. Why, I fell in myself just before you came and...well, see? I'm okay."

Joycie stood up, her clothes looking like they'd shrunk three sizes. Her belly hung out over the edge of her shorts.

They looked like two fat, drowned rats.

"You tried to drown us, Richards! You're going to pay for our clothes, and we're going to call the police and have you arrested!" Her eyes were bulging out of her fat, purple face.

Her brother piped up, "Yeah, Richards, you sneaked up behind us and pushed us down the hill and into the deep water. Right, Joycie?"

"Hurry, Jacob! Let's tell Mumzie what Richards did to us!"

They scurried back up the hill and out of sight. I stood there drenched to the skin, holding my fishin' pole. *Billy was right,* I thought. *I sure won't catch any more fish today.*

I headed home. As I reached the clearing by the pond, I saw Dr. Smith's car in our driveway. I had no sooner gotten halfway up the driveway when he came out the door carrying my mother, with Donna and Tommy walking beside them.

I dropped my fishin' pole and ran up the driveway. "What's the matter, Mother? Why can't you walk?"

Donna caught me in her arms. "It's all right, Boguidie. Mother needs to go get fixed up at the hospital. I'll take care of you till she gets home."

Dr. Smith gently put Mother in the passenger side of his car. Panic engulfed my whole body with the fear that my mother was going to die and I needed to save her.

I tore out of Donna's arms, ran to the car past the doctor, and pulled the door open on the driver's side. I jumped into the seat next to my mother. "You're not taking my mother anywhere without me!" I held onto her and glared up at the doctor.

Mother wrapped her arms around me. "Maureen, where have you been?" She smoothed my wet, tangled hair off my forehead. "You're soaking wet and full of mud."

"Come on, Boguidie, I have a special surprise for you," Donna said.

"I don't want any stupid surprise! I want my mom! She's not going to any goddamn hospital without me!"

Uncle David came flying out of Grampa's side of the house. Aunt Dora took her usual slow, deliberate steps, ready to take control of the situation as always.

Uncle David leaned into the car, pried me off my mother, and carried me kicking and screaming toward the house.

"Let me go, you bastard!"

"What you need, young lady, is a good spanking, and I'm the one to do it. Just listen to that mouth of yours."

He dropped me to the ground. I stumbled, but regained my balance.

"You goddamn son-of-a-bitchin' cock-sucken whore!" I'd heard my father level my mother with that string of cuss words, and by the beet-red flush on my uncle's cheeks, I knew my message had hit the mark. I felt the smash of the back of his hand across my face, sending me flying backwards to the ground.

Tommy came flying in from nowhere and grabbed me. He held me with both his arms wrapped so tight around me. I had to quit struggling. I just wanted to rip into my uncle, no matter how big he was. "Don't ever touch my little sister again! Look what you did! Her mouth is bleeding!" Tommy shouted, his fists clenched.

"What in the name of God is going on here?" Evidently, Aunt Dora had missed my verbal assault against Uncle David.

"Did you hear what she called me? I'd like to knock her teeth out."

"Just you try it, you big dumb jackass," I retaliated, as I struggled to free myself from Tommy's grip.

Aunt Dora cleared her throat before she spoke. "These kids are out of control."

Tommy loosened his grip. Seeing my chance to escape, I ripped free of his grasp and tore across the yard. I could hear Tommy's footfalls right behind me. I ran around to the back of the house, hit the basement steps, and flew into the cellar. Tommy joined me behind the furnace. He wrapped his arm around me. "It's okay, Maureen. I'll protect you."

The heating register above our heads echoed the conversation in the kitchen above our heads.

"I'm sick to death of these kids, and of Laura and her constant problems," Dora's voice rang through the cellar. "It's killing our mother."

"Enough is enough, Dora," Uncle David's voice shook.

There was a long silence, then Aunt Dora replied with, "They need to go back to the orphanage."

Tommy began to tremble.

"Why don't you take the kids until Laura gets on her feet?" David asked.

"I've been waiting for her to get on her feet for years. She was told not to go out that night. As far as I'm concerned, she got just what she asked for."

Tommy and I froze at the sound of footsteps on the cement floor.

"I thought I'd find you two down here," said Donna. "Are you okay, Boguidie? I hate Uncle David too. I don't know who he thinks he is, that he dare touch any of us." Big tears slid down my sister's face as she held me close to her.

"Dora and David said they were going to call someone or something 'cause they don't want to take care of us, and they might send us to the orphanage," I said. "I didn't go there, but I know all about you and Tommy and Ted going there. Who did that to you? I hate their guts."

"That will never happen to you, Boguidie, or to any of us again," Donna said firmly. "We're not so little that we can't take care of ourselves, so don't ever worry about that."

"But who took you there?"

Donna just held me to her. I could feel her sobs and warm tears on my cheek. Tommy came over to where we were standing and rubbed my sister's back.

"Boguidie, you were just a baby, so Dad left you with Mom and Gramma and Grampa," said Tommy. "He took me and Ted to Parmadale, and Donna to St. Joseph's Orphanage. We stayed there for two years and never saw you or Mom even one time."

The three of us held tight to each other and cried until there were no more tears left. There were so many questions in my mind. Why did our own father do that? How could anyone be so mean?

Donna was the first to speak.

"Oh, don't worry about Dora and David. They just come over here and get everyone upset, then leave. Anyway, my surprise is that you get to get a permanent at Mrs. Bensen's beauty parlor tomorrow. What do you think of that?"

"Does it hurt? I'll do it if it don't hurt," I said.

"I promise it won't hurt. You'll look beautiful for when Mother comes home from the hospital on Wednesday. Let's go down to the creek and pick some violets for Mother. By the time we finish, Dora and David will be gone."

The three of us walked down to the creek and over to Sydney Smith's hill to pick three huge bouquets of flowers for our mother. Donna was right. By the time we got back home, the "enemy," as Tommy called them, were gone. We all pitched in and cleaned up the house; and, as usual, when we finished cleaning we rearranged all the furniture.

"Boy, the house sure looks beautiful. What are we going to have for supper, Donna?" I opened the old oak icebox, which contained an onion, some dried-up celery, and half a quart of milk. "The ice is almost all gone, but don't worry, the ice man comes tomorrow. Want me to pick some fresh corn for supper, Donna?"

"Good idea, Boguidie. We'll have some buttered noodles with it."

We ate our dinner together and enjoyed every morsel. Tommy was on his good behavior and didn't tease me once. We listened to our programs and turned in early. I curled up next to my sister as she tucked the thin blanket around my back.

"Donna, tell me again about Hansel and Gretel and the mean stepmother."

"Once upon a time, there was a sister and brother -- Hansel and Gretel, were their names -- who lived in a little cottage..."

Donna stopped at the sound of someone, or something, falling down the basement stairs. Tommy, being the closest one to that door, flew out of bed and slid the bolt lock into the latch. It was pitch dark. All I could hear was my heart pounding in my ears. A beam of light shot across Donna and me.

"Psst, it's all right. It's me, Grampa. Stay right where you are and don't turn on any lights."

Grampa's flashlight glanced off Tommy in his underwear, holding Mother's rolling pin. He followed Grampa, who was in his union suit, sporting a baseball bat. They disappeared around the back of the house. The stairway light flipped on, and the old coats, hats, and junk that lined the steps cast an array of eerie shadows on the wall. Donna and I sprang from our bed and ran to the basement door just in time to hear Grampa's voice.

"What in the hell do ya think you're doin'?"

Eddie O'Keefe, one of the bindelstiffs that lived at Avon Isle Dance Hall, lay at the foot of the stairs. He had on the same wrinkled, navy-blue suit he'd been wearing every day for years.

Eddie struggled to sit up. "Oh, I see. I must have gotten turned around a wee bit. I was just enjoying me first quart of beer over at the pond."

Grampa helped him sit on the step, remarking, "Sounds like John Barleycorn has finally gotten to your brain, Eddie. Why, I almost parted your hair with this ball bat, ya crazy old fool."

"Aye, sorry if I startled ya. By the time I finished the second -- or was it the third? -- quart over at the pond, I guess I got turned around following that big pink elephant." Chuckling at his wit, he waved an arm in my direction. "I was just thinkin' about the wee one over there pullin' those two fat little pigs out of the drink, I was." He chuckled and scratched his head.

Grampa spoke up. "Well, let's get you out to the road and head you in the right direction back to the hall, Eddie. You need to think about givin' up the drink. When you start seeing things like pigs in the pond, it's time to quit." No one knew what Eddie was talking about but I sure did. He must have seen the whole thing at the pond with Joycie and Jacob.

Grampa and Tommy each took old Eddie by an arm and ushered him back out to Stoney Ridge as Donna and I sat on the porch and supervised the whole operation.

Grandpa reappeared, leaning on the bat like it was a cane. "I think we've had enough excitement for one night. I just might catch a chill running around in my drawers like this, so let's all get back to bed before Henry starts crowing." Grampa stepped through the doorway and disappeared into his side of the house.

I eyed my brother. "Hey, Tommy, how'd you get the rolling pin so fast, anyways?"

"I'll tell you guys if you promise not to laugh. I sleep with the rolling pin under my bed. Just about the time I was thinking it was dumb, I needed it."

"When did you start doing that?"

"When Ted joined the Air Force. After he left, I used to lay awake at night hearing every noise in the house and wondering what I would do if someone broke in. So I just got up one night and got Mother's rolling pin. Sometimes I just get so scared and feel like I'm just going to die or something. Do you ever feel like that?"

I knew exactly what he meant, and felt tremendous relief to hear I was not the only one who had experienced that crazy feeling in my chest. "I call those 'scared spells,' Tommy, and I get them a lot. I don't even know what I'm scared of, but it's the worst feeling in the world."

The three of us all slept in Mother's bed the rest of that night.

# # #

I woke up to the smell of toast and coffee. Donna had poured our mostly-milk coffee and made toast with the last of the bread.

"Are you ready for your permanent, Boguidie?" she asked. "Mrs. Benson is expecting you in a half-hour, so you better finish eating and get dressed."

I dunked my toast in my coffee, took two bites, and got dressed.

Donna ran a comb through my hair, saying, "I'll walk you over there. Then I have to leave to go clean house for Mrs. Tomlan."

We started on down the line to Mrs. Benson's beauty shop, just around the corner from John and Jean's and past Avon Isle Park.

"I'm really glad I'm getting a permanent," I said, "because if it's all curly, I'll never need to comb it, right?"

"No, dear heart, you'll still need to comb it. It'll just look really cute, and you'll be all ready for school then." Donna glanced up and stiffened, clutching my hand tighter as we walked. "Oh, no, here comes Eddie O'Keefe. Just walk past him."

"That's not very nice, Donna. He's really a nice old man. He's just a little dirty, that's all, and down on his luck."

Eddie approached, grinning at us and showing spaces where several teeth should've been. "Well, top of the mornin' t' ya, ladies. I'm a little down on me luck. Ya' wouldn't happen t' have any spare change for a cup of coffee for old Eddie, would ya?"

I reached into my pocket and pulled out a nickel. "Here you go, Eddie."

"Little lass, it's you. How's your fishin' goin' these days?" He bent down, and his breath smelled like an empty beer bottle. His blue eyes twinkled like he was about to say something, but he thought better of it and just winked.

Then he danced his way to Kaiser's Tavern, singing, "Now Ireland be Ireland when England was just a pup, and Ireland be Ireland when England just grew up. I am an Irish citizen and go t' Sunday mass, and every English son-of-a-bitch can kiss me Irish ass!" Opening the tavern's screen door, he made his grand entrance. With a smile on my face, I watched as Eddie made his hellos around the bar. *I just love him,* I thought.

Donna talked to me with a strange fierceness to her voice. "Maureen Ann Richards, now you listen to me. What are you doing talking to that old bum like he's your long-lost friend? Why, he could kidnap you or you could catch almost anything from just standing next to him. From now on, I want to know whenever you change direction. An adult needs to know exactly where you are, and you don't go past John and Jean's or near Avon Isle Park and the bindelstiffs."

"But Donna, he's just a nice old man, and I love the way he talks."

"You heard me, Boguidie."

Donna took me into the beauty shop, talked to Mrs. Bensen about my hair, and then left for work. I sat in the chair and watched as Mrs. Bensen wound my hair up in curlers with white paper on each one. After my whole head was covered in thin metal curlers, she methodically squeezed solution onto each one. The fumes were enough to choke a horse. After sitting under the dryer for an eternity, Mrs. Bensen combed out the tight curls that covered my head. I went from looking bald to instant frizz.

She clasped her hands together and beamed at me. "Now don't you look just adorable. Why, you look just like Shirley Temple."

I looked in the mirror. "Are you sure my hair is supposed to stand out like that? It looks goofy to me." She stepped back in order to get a better look.

"Well, it's just a little tight. It will look better after you wash it a few times, dear."

I went home along the creek, instead of along the street where everyone could see me. *Donna will know what to do with this hair,* I kept reassuring myself.

I spent the rest of the day in and out of the bathroom, catching glimpses of myself from every angle in the mirror until I was feeling that my hair was okay. When I walked into the kitchen, Tommy had just come in from his paper route.

He stood and looked at me. "What happened to your hair? Did Br'er Fox catch you and think you were the Tar Baby?"

"Mrs. Benson said I look like Shirley Temple, so just you shut up. Anyway, you're just jealous."

"Well, look at it this way. If you ever need money, you can just get sheared and sell all that wool to a rug factory. Or, better yet, you could pass for Gravel Girdie."

That was it. I flew at my brother, swinging my fists.

He grabbed me and held onto my fists for dear life. "Oh, my God, take it easy! I'm just kidding! You look like a girl, not Gravel Girdie."

I knew he was talking about the wild-haired lady in the *Dick Tracy* comics. He finally let loose of me, and I stood and glared at him. I really wanted to cry, but that was something I had vowed never to do again.

"God, who needs a guard dog with you in the house?" He quickly added, "Just kidding," before he walked away.

Donna finally got home, and, as usual, took care of my hair and my injured ego, saying, "Everyone will be so surprised at how cute your hair is, Boguidie. Mother's coming home tomorrow, and she will be so happy when she sees your hair."

Of course, we were all excited, and we cleaned and rearranged all the furniture for the second time since Mother had entered the hospital. I dove into bed with the same anticipation I felt on Midnight Mass on Christmas Eve. My mom was coming home, and everything was going to be better now.

# # #

The next morning, Grampa drove Donna, Tommy, and me to St. Joseph's Hospital to get our mother.

"Them hair surely does look nice, little Maureen." Grampa kept looking in the rearview mirror at my new hairdo.

"Thanks, Grampa. I smell good, too."

Donna kept poking Tommy every time he looked like he wanted to say something.

We arrived at the hospital, and had to wait in the car for Grampa to bring Mother out. Finally, Grampa stepped out of the orange-brick building with a nurse pushing a wheelchair holding our mother.

"I thought they were going to fix her," I said. "Look, she still can't walk."

I had no sooner gotten the words out of my mouth when Grampa helped Mother to her feet, saying, "Tommy, open the door for your mother."

Jumping out of the back seat, Tommy held the door open to the passenger side of the old four-door sedan.

Mother slowly stood up out of the wheelchair and cautiously slid into the front seat, holding her stomach with one hand.

I stretched my arms over the back of her seat and gently wrapped my arms around her neck. I tilted my head to try to see her face and show her my hair. Her eyes had such dark circles around them, I thought for sure she was even sicker.

Even so, I had to ask, "Are you all better, Mother?"

She lowered her head into her hands and barely answered my question. "I just want to go home."

The ride back was silent. Grampa drove, and the three of us stared out the window. We pulled into the driveway, and

Grampa slowed the car to a stop. I looked over at Dunker's house to see if Mrs. Dunker had taken her shift looking out the window, monitoring the goings-on at the Richards' household. And there she stood, gawking out the small window that overlooked our house. I gave an 'I-see-you-there' wave, and she disappeared from sight.

All four of us helped Mother out of the car and into the house. We made our way to the bedroom, where Donna held back the covers for her and said, "I just washed the sheets so it would be all fresh for you."

Once Mother was in bed, Donna gently covered her up and tucked the covers around her back. A fly zoomed around the bed and landed on the covers. I promptly recruited the fly swatter from the top of the icebox and went to kill it before it bothered Mother. I crept slowly up within striking distance, and swatted it with all the strength I could muster.

Mother cried out in pain as I killed the predator, because I had hit her stomach in doing so. I wanted to die on the spot. Donna grabbed my arm.

"Oh my God, Maureen! What are you doing?"

"I killed the fly."

She gave me an exasperated look and said, "Why don't you go out and fish or something?"

It wasn't an order, but it felt like it, so I obeyed. Walking over to Billy's house, I felt like someone had punched me in the stomach. By the time I arrived at his back door, I tried to sing out for Billy in the most cheerful voice I could muster, so as not to let on that I really felt like crying.

"Oh, Billy, can you come out to play?"

"I'm back here, Maureen."

Billy waved from the strawberry patch, where he stood holding a basket full of berries. There were rows and rows of strawberries with baskets piled at the end of each row. Some of the ladies from church, with their big straw hats on, were picking the berries, along with some big kids. The little kids were not allowed in the patch because Mrs. Smith said that what they didn't step on, they ate.

"Hi, Billy. Good morning, Mrs. Smith."

She looked at me from under a huge straw hat and smiled from where she stood, under an apple tree, sorting berries, all her fingers stained red.

I continued, "Look how tall I am. I think I'm finally big enough to pick this year."

Mrs. Smith arched an eyebrow. "You do, do ya? Well, just look at your hair. Now that's more like it. What do you think of Maureen's hair, Billy?"

My friend stared, clutching his basket. "What happened to your hair? You look like a *girl*!"

Mrs. Smith and all the ladies in the berry patch were looking at me and laughing. Mrs. Smith walked around the table she was working at and put her hand on my shoulder. "I think what Billy means is, it looks real nice. Right, Billy?"

"Yeah, it looks real nice."

"So, you want to be a picker. Well, let me see just how tall you are." She held up her hand to the top of my head. I straightened up as tall as I could, holding my breath to make myself even taller.

"Well, yes, by golly, I do think you are big enough. Come day after tomorrow, and bring your lunch and your straw hat. I pay ten cents a basket, but only pick the red ones."

"I'll be here for sure. And I'll go to Buck's Hardware for my hat this afternoon. Thanks, Mrs. Smith. I gotta go tell my mother. See ya later, Billy."

My excitement was short-lived, however, as I crossed the street and saw the Schmidts' white Cadillac parked in our driveway. Being an eternal optimist, my heart skipped a beat, thinking they probably came to thank me for helping their kids out of the pond. My mind didn't stop there. I figured probably all would be forgiven, and they would like me and invite me to their house to play.

I opened the door. Mrs. Schmidt sat on the flowered chair with Jacob and Joycie flanked on either side of her. One look at her face, with those same bulging eyes she had unfortunately passed on to her daughter, snapped me back to reality.

Those rats! I thought. *I should have left them shift for themselves instead of helping them.* The words of John the bakery delivery man echoed in my head: *"Who would believe you, anyhow?"*

I sat down on a corner of the chair, avoiding the exposed spring in the middle of the cushion, and faced her glare.

"I don't think what you did today to Joycie and Jacob was very nice. In fact, they could have drowned. Why did you push them into the pond?"

"They lied. They fell in, and I helped them out."

Grampa and Gramma looked at one another in utter disbelief.

Gramma then said sharply to me, "They are good children like you should be. You should be like them and not tell lies."

Mrs. Schmidt nodded in agreement with my grandmother, adding, "The whole town knows her and the wild devil she is. Can't you do something with her before she really hurts someone? Let alone our children picking up swear words?"

Joycie and Jacob grinned and nodded with a look of pure satisfaction. I couldn't stand another minute of their smirking faces, and shouted, "Tell your mother the truth! You were throwing mud clumps at me and rolled down the hill into the pond! I even helped your butts out of the water!"

They edged behind their mother for protection, which was the smartest thing they had done all day. All I wanted to do was smack them into next week. I looked at my grandfather.

"What about Eddie O'Keefe, Grampa? He told you what happened. He was there."

Mrs. Schmidt's mouth fell open in utter disbelief. "Oh, my dear Lord! Now she wants the town drunk to lie for her. Come, children. I must have taken leave of my senses to come here in the first place."

Gramma grabbed my arm, hissing, "Tell them you are sorry." Her eyes burned into mine. Guess Johnny the pee-pee pastry man was right.

I stepped around Mrs. Schmidt to face the enemy. "Sorry. That is, sorry I didn't let you two fat little jackasses drown."

Mrs. Schmidt frantically reached to cover their ears and usher them out the door all at the same time. In her haste, her toe caught in the hole of the rug, sending the three of them falling out the door and sprawling out on the porch. Grampa was at their side in an instant, helping Mrs. Schmidt up, and I thought I could see a suppressed grin starting at the corners of his mouth. I stood with my arms crossed, grinning from ear to ear, and said, "I think Jesus is trying to tell you something."

The perfect mother hustled her perfect children out of reach, mumbling and looking over her shoulder to make sure I was not going to launch another attack.

After they left, Gramma took a firm grip on the wheel of her wheelchair to spin around in utter disgust at my dreadful behavior. Her mutterings trailed after her, and burned a painful scar in my heart.

I took off for the Butternut Tree to try to make sense out of the usual nonsense of life at 2788 Stoney Ridge Road.

CHAPTER FIVE

First Grade and Sister Mary Daniel

"I love you, Dear Jesus. I love you, my dear. I will love you and love you each day of the year."

-- Sister Mary Daniel

The warm summer days became shorter, and the once-green leaves of the oaks and maple trees turned the most beautiful blended shades of crimson and yellow-orange. At the end of each driveway, neatly raked piles of leaves either smoldered or were ready to be burned. The air was thick with the rich fragrance of the burning leaves.

The order from the Sears and Roebuck Catalog had arrived, containing my school clothes. There were three pairs of white cotton underpants with cotton short-sleeved undershirts to match. One red-plaid pinafore and one blue dress with a Peter

Pan collar and puffy sleeves would be my wardrobe for the school year.

The brown leather high-tops I so desperately wanted couldn't be ordered for lack of money, so I polished my old ones, one of which had the sole that flapped as I walked. They did not have the coveted hooks at the top for the laces like Billy's shoes had, but they kind of looked like his.

The brisk fall air was filled with excitement with the return of the nuns to the convent from their summer retreat. The big question was: Who I would get for my teacher?

We played in the schoolyard every day, hoping to get a glimpse of the sisters, and to see if Sister Mary Daniel was back. Finally, the night before the first day of school, I was soaking in my usual inch of lukewarm bath water when I decided I was right next to being a grown-up. I lathered up my leg, grabbed the Gillette Blue-Blade Razor that was sitting on the edge of the tub gathering rust, and took a grand swipe up my leg to shave off the peach fuzz.

Blood and stinging pain bloomed in its wake.

"Hey, Donna, I think I've killed myself! Hurry!"

I had taken off the first layer of skin from the ankle to my knee. Donna hurried in to see what trouble I could have possibly gotten into in the tub.

"It's okay, Boguidie. Let's put some toilet paper on it till it stops bleeding."

My sister never ceased to amaze me. She could fix anything. She continued, "Let's put your hair up in rag curls for the first day of school tomorrow."

She wrapped a towel around me as I got out of the tub. I quickly dried off, careful not to touch my leg, and pulled a tattered nightie over my head.

Thank God the perm had grown out. Donna got out an old white flour sack used as a dishtowel, tore it into strips, and parted my wet hair on the side. After dipping the comb into the jar of Dr. Ellis Green Hair Setting Gel, she used it to part my hair in sections. Holding one end of the strip at the part, she wrapped the hair tightly around it and tied the ends together. By the time we finished, my head was completely covered in rag curls.

"I can't wait till school tomorrow," I said. "I'm gonna meet Billy on the steps, and we're gonna sit by each other."

Tommy was sitting on the floor, folding his papers for his paper route.

"Hey Ma!" he shouted. "Ya better stay right outside of the school door, 'cause you know it's just a matter of time before the nun ticks her off and she starts to cuss."

"I don't say bad words anymore," I said huffily. "That was just when I was a little kid and didn't know any better. Besides, I love Sister Mary Daniel, and she'll like me better if I don't say any bad words. Right, Mother?"

Mother had been feeling better lately, and it showed in how she neatened herself up, these days, her hair pulled back sleek with a comb on either side of her face. She stood at the stove, slicing dough into the boiling water for dumplings, and shook her head at Tommy's and my bickering.

"Tommy, don't bully her. She'll do just fine with Sister Mary Daniel."

Feeling bold in the shadow of Mother's defense, I dared to ask, "Mother, it's been so long since I heard you sing, will you sing the song you wrote about the bird?"

"Oh, that old thing? All right. You get out the strainer so I can drain off the dumplings, and I'll sing."

As I rattled around, looking for the strainer, Mother's beautiful soprano voice filled our little kitchen: "The birdie that told me continues to scold me. He's way high up in a tree. I know that it's love dear; it's got to be love dear. Can't you see? 'Cause the birdie that told me."

I pulled out the old metal strainer from under the sink and checked it for mouse turds. I put it in the sink and asked, "Can you teach me to sing 'You Are My Sunshine' with you and Donna? I want to sing like you, Mother. Your voice is so beautiful."

She stopped stirring the dumplings for a minute and got that faraway look in her eyes. "When I was young, and your father and I were first married, we sang every Jeanette McDonald and Nelson Eddie song ever written. Your father had the most beautiful tenor voice. Oh, those were the days." She sighed, then shook herself back to the present. "Now all we need is some butter and salt and pepper."

We all sat down at our table by the kitchen window, and marveled at the huge green bowl filled to the top with steaming dumplings. The chips on the edge of the bowl went unnoticed in the presence of such bounty. It was just the perfect dinner on the night before the first day of school, and I didn't hold back on taking as many as I could eat.

After dinner, I went off to bed, too full to do anything but sleep.

# # #

Henry crowed, and I flew out of bed across the cold linoleum floor to sit in front of the heat register in my underwear and stare into space until I woke up. I don't know how long I sat there before I realized no heat was coming out. It was only September, and Grampa didn't start the coal furnace until the first frost was on the ground. I looked out the window and, sure enough, the overgrown grass was white with frost.

Grampa stuck his head around the corner and looked at me for a minute, then finally took his pipe out of his mouth and said, "Come sit here by the stove and Grampa will start the oven ta warm ya up, little Maureen. You've got a big day, and we wouldn't want t' start ya off on the wrong foot, no sir-eee."

I scurried over to the stove and basked in the warmth for a few minutes. Then I sprang into action, putting on the school clothes Donna had carefully laid out on a kitchen chair for me. My sister, still in her night-clothes, stood in the doorway supervising. "As soon as you finish dressing, we'll comb out your hair, Boguidie," she yawned.

Donna took out my rag curls and combed each one around her finger to form long sausage curls all around my head, while I sipped my coffee and dunked my toast.

"All done. And look how nice you look." She held up her hand mirror for my final inspection.

"Okay, I'm ready."

Donna leaned and gave me a hug. Then I ran into the bedroom to show Mother.

She was asleep, so I bounced back into the kitchen through the bathroom and opened the door to Gramma and Grampa's side of the house. Gramma looked up from eating her usual poached egg, and gave an approving nod.

"How do I look, Gramma?" I stood beside her for approval. She wiped her mouth, leaving some egg on her chin. I picked up the napkin and wiped it off for her.

"Why, don't you just look dandy?" She smiled. "Now, just be a good girl and don't say bad words." She held both of my hands and gently shook them for emphasis.

"I won't ever say them again, Gramma. I promise."

The long strip of skin, from my ankle to my knee, was still raw and held pieces of toilet paper -- evidence of my encounter with the razor the night before. My old brown oxfords had been well-polished, but the turned-up toes held deep creases from the shoes being two sizes too large.

Lassie stood by the front door, wagging her tail and ready for another day of following my every step from the pond to the creek and anything in between. But that had been summer. This was a school day.

"You have to stay here, girl," I said.

She thumped her tail enthusiastically.

I sighed. "Well, come on then. I know you'll follow me anyways, and you can wait outside for me under the maples." With that, the two of us took off for school.

Dick and Don Wagner stood in front of the school steps with their little brother Jake. Dick shouted, "Hey, Richards, where'd ya get the new clothes?"

"From the Sears Roebuck Catalog. Where'd ya get yours?" I retorted.

He looked me up one side and down the other. Then he started in on the same old questions, plus some new ones. "Do you ever see your dad? Where's he at, anyway? Look at those shoes. Didn't you have enough money for new ones?"

I looked down at my shoes. Except for the sole flapping, they really looked good all polished up.

Don stepped in front of his brother. "Shut up, Dick." He turned to me. "You look real nice, Maureen. Be sure and tell Donna I said hello."

"Oh, I will. I just love watching her face when I tell her everything you two say. She always looks like she just smelled something really bad."

The air was brisk with patches of frost on the school grounds. Heavy clouds threatened rain or snow. This was really early for this kind of weather, and none of us were dressed for it. The wind swirled around my bare legs and sent a shiver up my spine. I clutched my red sweater together where it was missing a button. The schoolyard was covered with the leaves from the huge maples.

Kids ran through the leaves, playing tag, until Sister Mary Adorika appeared on the steps of the school, ringing her brass hand bell. Everyone froze in their spots, and poor little Jimmy Brader wet his pants.

"I vant da first graders here in front of der steps." The door creaked opened. "Sister Mary Daniel vill take you to your class."

Sister Mary Daniel stepped out of the doorway with the same sweet smile she always wore on her very young face. "Follow me, children."

I had not seen Billy come up behind me.

"Hi, Maureen," he whispered. "Think I'd rather go turtle-hunting. My neck is itching like crazy in this goofy shirt." He tugged at his starched white shirt.

His new blue denim dungarees were held up with a belt that was three sizes too big. As usual, his hair was plastered down on either side of a crooked part, and the shine on his nose only accented his freckles. Grimy little-boy hands stuck out of white cuffs, fingernails bitten down to the quick.

"Yeah, but at least we got Sister Mary Daniel," I responded.

It started to rain as we lined up in front of the steps. As I stood there, I could feel my sock getting wet from the gaping hole in the bottom of my shoe. *No matter,* I thought. *They look good on top.*

We filed into the front hallway. The dark-oak wainscoting covered the wall halfway up. Light-green enamel paint with thick drip lines went up to a high ceiling covered in tan water-stain.

We walked straight ahead, across the shiny wood-planked floor, to Sister Mary Daniel's first and second grade classroom. The room was divided in half by rows of desks. They were separated, with one section for the first grade and the other for the second. The second-grade desks were easy to spot -- they had inkwells. The first-grade desks did not, because only second graders could use real ink pens.

The room was painted the same light-green as the hall, and three tall rectangular windows punctuated the outside wall. Sister Mary Daniel's desk faced the class, with a semicircle of little, dark wood chairs for the reading group off to one side. The gray slate blackboard faced the class, the alphabet chalked across the top. The three-foot-long rubber-tipped pointer hung beside the flag in a corner. The old iron steam heaters hissed and sputtered as we found our desks with Sister's help. She tapped the bell on her desk twice. Silence fell over the room.

"Second graders, I'm going to ask you to help in the pledge and morning prayer until the first graders learn to say it."

We all followed in our best "sing-song" voices in the pledge, with our hands held reverently over our hearts. Second-grader Marie Little stood beside her front-row desk, looking back at us, giggling and gawking at us first-year students.

After the pledge, Sister introduced the morning prayer. "Boys and girls, I wrote a very special morning prayer to Jesus that we will be saying together every morning. Ready? One...two...three. 'Good morning, dear Jesus. Good morning, my dear. I will love you and love you each day of the year."

Prayer done, Sister tapped her bell. The second graders sat down and we followed suit. I sat down in the heavy wood seat, running one tentative finger over the black, wrought-iron armrests shaped into thick scrolls. The seats folded down from the back, and were joined together to form one row. The desk was bolted to the floor by the same black wrought iron. The desktop lifted from the front to reveal a well for our books, papers, and pencils.

The far corner of the classroom held the tall oak doors that led to the cloakroom. My brother Tommy told me never to go in there, because he knew of kids who went in and never came out.

Sister Mary Daniel cleared her throat. "Children, starting with the first grade, row one, you may take your lunches and wraps to the cloakroom, if need be."

You may be Sister Mary Daniel and all, I thought, *but no way in hell am I going into* that *room.* I raised my hand.

"Yes, Maureen, you have a question?"

I stood up beside my desk. "I'm going home for lunch. Do I still need to line up?"

Marie Little covered her mouth and began to giggle. Without even looking at her, Sister said, "Marie, do you have something funny to share with the class?"

"Oh, no, Sister, it's okay," she said, just above a whisper.

Get her, Sister! I thought. Marie was standing beside her desk. *Pee your pants! Just pee your pants!* I yelled in my head.

Finally, under Sister's calm stare, Marie admitted, "I said that Richards probably didn't even own a coat to hang up." The class laughed, and Sister tapped her bell three times.

"Now, Marie," she said reproachfully. "Would Jesus say that to one of his friends? I think you need to write 'I will be kind to all of my friends, rich or poor,' ten times on the blackboard, at recess."

Billy leaned forward and whispered in my ear, "If I had a nose like hers, I'd use it for a fishing pole."

Billy really did say the best stuff. He saved me from walking over there and punching Marie a good one. *Just wait till I see her on the playground,* I promised myself.

That morning, we each got to stand up and say our full name and draw a picture of our family. I carefully drew my mom, Donna, and Tommy, and left a space for my father, just in case he ever came back.

I couldn't take my eyes off Chucky Buldoff, a fellow first-grader. He had thick brown curly hair, big blue eyes, and a wet chin. He drooled nonstop as he colored his paper all in black crayon. His gramma was the old gray-haired lady my brother had nicknamed "Gallstones." At home, Tommy liked to imitate her looking for something in her purse. He'd stick his whole head in one of Mother's old purses and dig.

Chucky sat up in his chair and grinned at me with the biggest toothless grin I'd ever seen. *Now I know why everyone calls him "Toothless,"* I thought.

The morning half over, Sister tapped her bell, and everyone stood up for recess. She opened the heavy oak door, and we all filed out onto the playground. An iron fire escape led down from the second floor, where the fifth and sixth grades shared one room and the seventh and eighth grades shared yet another. The square iron support for the fire escape made the ideal "jail" for a good game of "jailbreak."

I seized the opportunity to catch Marie Little and knock her flat into a mud puddle -- all in the name of good fun. Later, Sister came out onto the playground, ringing her brass bell for us to line up to use the lavatory.

The lavatory was a separate brick building divided in half -- one side for the girls and the other for the boys. I could smell the stench before I ever walked in there. Tommy had advised me to hold my breath and pee fast. Five years older than me, he was in the sixth grade and all-too-familiar with that lavatory. Inside, a row of dark oak toilet seats crouched over a deep trench. Tommy was right. I went to the bathroom double-quick, without taking a breath; but I could still smell the stench, which made my eyes water.

Before I knew it, it was lunchtime, and I found myself skipping down the dirt path, covered with wet maple leaves, the sole of my shoe flapping in the breeze. I could smell Mother's fresh bread baking as I rounded the corner of the long, cindered driveway leading up to our front porch. I flung open the screen door and pounced into the living room, all in one motion.

Mother was at the stove, slicing bread.

She wasn't alone.

My father sat at the kitchen table with a glass of whiskey in one hand.

I stopped in my tracks and said a silent prayer to the Blessed Mother for finally hearing my prayer and bringing my dad home -- to stay, this time.

CHAPTER SIX

The Old Man

"What so ever you do to the least of my children, you do unto me."

-- Matthew 25:40

My father greeted me with, "Well, what did you do today to earn the ground you're standing on?"

My throat was too dry to answer, even if I had known what he was talking about. I walked past him to my mother and leaned up against her leg to face my dad. Instead of answering him, I blurted out, "Are you gonna stay home with us now and not leave anymore?"

He took a gulp of his drink before answering. "Where do you get off asking a question like that? Don't you know kids are to be seen and not heard?"

I turned around and buried my face in my mother's dress, determined not to let him see me cry. *I wish Eddie O'Keefe was my dad,* I thought. *He may be the town drunk, but at least he's nice to me.*

I grabbed a slice of bread off the stove. My dad's eyes were on me as I squared my shoulders, jerked the weathered storm door open, and stepped outside. Feeling sick to my stomach, I looked down at the thick slice of bread and stuck it in the pocket of my red sweater. The wind was picking up, and a few scattered snow flurries landed on my cheeks. Lassie appeared out of nowhere, like she always did. We followed the old frozen dirt path past the half-falling-down chicken coop to my Butternut Tree.

The frozen bank felt cold on my fanny, but it was my heart that hurt the most. I pulled my knees tight to my chest and buried my face in my arms. My dog stood guard at my side.

Now it was safe to cry. *Why is he so damn mean?* I questioned over and over in my mind. Then panic struck in the middle of my stomach. *What if he hurts my mom?* I stood up and wiped the tears off my face. *No,* I reassured myself. *I'm sure this time will be different. I'll bet he didn't mean to hurt my feelings, and this time he'll stay and learn how to be a nice dad. I'll stop swearing and we will be a real family and go to church together and sit in the family section.* I breathed a sigh of relief. Everything was going to be just fine...

Boy, it sure was cold. I noticed that ice had formed in the water. "Ice skating!" I shouted. Upon further inspection, I saw that the ice was solid at the edges of the water but barely frozen in the middle.

My attention was distracted by a duck waddling along the bank of the creek, beak to the ground, searching for any stray, frozen worms. If I caught him, maybe we could have a nice dinner with Dad, Mom, Tommy, and Donna.

"Grampa said the good Lord gave us chickens to eat, and you're almost a chicken," I whispered.

I stood still, not moving a muscle. A vision of hot mashed potatoes, steaming gravy, and mouthwatering meat on our table danced through my brain. I was really hungry and couldn't remember the last time I'd had meat. To me, at that moment, it seemed that the duck would solve all my problems and fill my stomach, as well.

I dove for him. He flapped his wings, intent on escape, feet skating across the ice.

I was right on his tail and grabbed him by the head. We slid into the bank of the creek together, feathers flying in my face, beak quacking loud in my ears. I stood and swung him around, his wings frantically flapping until...he stopped moving.

I dropped him to the ground. He was dead. I stared in disbelief at the limp body, then knelt down, afraid to touch it.

"I'm so sorry, duck."

I sobbed so hard that I threw up. After that, I pulled myself together, and hunted down frozen leaves and sticks on the riverbank to cover its body.

Lassie just sat in front of me, wagging her tail, as I performed the little ceremony.

When the duck could no longer be seen below the debris, I turned to my dog. "Come on, girl. Let's get out of here," I said, turning my back on the nightmare that just happened. Taking slow, deliberate steps, trying to justify my crime to get the sick feeling out of my guts, I heard a familiar voice.

"Maureen what are you up to?" I looked up and there stood Rose, my lady friend. The lump that had settled in my throat made it impossible to answer. Rose dropped her collection of orange bittersweet branches and took a few quick steps to get to me. She took my face in her hands. Try as I might, the tears refused to stop running down my face. Embarrassed, I buried my face in her thick wool jacket and sobbed.

Rose held me close and waited to speak. When I finally caught my breath she said, "Well, first of all, you're soaking wet and shivering cold, so let's take care of that." Struggling to regain my composure, I slowly pulled my face out of the comfort of her chest to look up at her. Retrieving a hanky from her pocket, she gently wiped my face and whispered, "Let's get out of here and go to my house for some nice warm soup." I took deep breaths as we walked toward her house. Rose lived just two houses down from Grampa's farm, along the creek with her husband Nick.

"I sure hope you haven't given up on teaching me how to ice skate, Maureen. I didn't do so good last year. The ice melted before you had a chance to show me how to go backwards."

She made me feel so much better that I was glad I had showed her all my secret places on my creek. "It sure feels like winter is back, Rose. The pond and creek will freeze soon and I will help you learn to skate really good."

Two friends, one big and one little, followed the worn path that led to Rose's back door.

The fireplace, stacked with burning logs, was crackling as we stepped into her tidy kitchen. Rose went straight over to an overstuffed green chair, pushed it in front of the hearth, and sat me down in it. Pulling off my boots and soaked socks, she then tucked the blanket that had been on the back of the chair all around me. Satisfied that she was making progress, she sat back on her heels and said, "I hope that someday I have a little girl just like you."

Still in her jacket and boots, she went over to her stove and struck a match to light the burner under a pot of soup. She went back to the door, took off her boots, and hung up her jacket on one of the two brass hooks there. I sat rubbing my toes together watching her prepare our lunch. As the soup steamed, she cut thick slices of bread on a cutting board, then got a saucer of butter from the icebox. After carefully lathering the fresh baked bread with butter, she poured the rich tomato soup into flowered bowls. "Now we feast," she said as she carefully arranged our lunch on a tray and brought it to a small round table that sat between us.

This is how I will live when I grow up, I thought.

"A penny for your thoughts, Maureen."

I dunked my bread into the steaming hot soup. It was so good, so warm. When the huge slice of bread was gone and the last drop of the rich tomato liquid slid down my throat, I looked over at my Rose.

"Better?" she inquired.

I sat my empty bowl on the tray and wrapped tighter in my blanket.

"Will you still be my friend if I tell you what I did?" I asked. Not waiting for an answer, I needed to continue before I lost my nerve. "I ran to my Butternut Tree because my dad came back home and he's drinking whiskey in my kitchen and being mean. I pray every night and at my Butternut Tree that he will come home and stay for good." I paused to swallow my tears that wanted to come, then continued.

"I was just sitting on the bank under my tree when I saw a duck waddling towards me. I thought if I could catch it we could eat it. I could see me and my whole family sitting down to a Sunday dinner together just like a real family."

Rose cleared her throat and looked down at the floor. I wiped my nose on my sleeve, and took a breath to get my courage up to finish the worst part of what I needed to tell her.

"My Grampa told me that God made chickens for us to eat and, well, I figured that a duck is almost a chicken. I just didn't know how awful it would feel to kill it."

Rose blew her nose in her hanky as I searched her face for the verdict.

"You and your Grampa are both right. God gives us chickens and ducks to eat. I completely understand what happened and would feel the same way. Thank you for telling me what was hurting you so badly. We will be friends forever, no matter what."

I stood and peeled off the warm blanket.

"I have to go home now and make sure my mom is okay. I hope he never comes back. I hate his guts! Actually, he can come home when he stops drinking the 'John Barleycorn' and he is not mean and drunk."

Rose walked me to the door. After I put on my sweater and boots, she opened the door and said, "You are right, Maureen, and I am on your side."

Once I was outside, the cool air felt good as I made my way back home. I whispered a prayer to the Blessed Mother. "Sorry for hurting the duck and thank you for my Rose, dear Lady."

I snuck through the basement door unannounced, deciding I'd see if everything was all clear before letting everyone know I was home. It took a few minutes for my eyes to get used to the dark. Lassie walked over to the coal furnace and curled up to get warm.

The stairs up to the kitchen were lined with old boots and shoes all the way to the top. Above the railings, nails punctuated the walls and held Grampa's many pairs of coveralls. I made my way over to the wringer washing machine, above which dangled a single light bulb. My fingers found the long string and, with a flick of my wrist, a dim light illuminated the dust-covered cement floor.

Grampa's fruit cellar was in the corner, behind a handmade door that hung cockeyed on the wall. I entered the small, damp room and went in search of an apple in the large, wood barrel. Grabbing a weathered apple off the top, I took a bite. Despite the wrinkled skin, it was juicy and sweet.

Wind whistled through the cellar door. I could see through the cracked window that the sun was setting behind billowing gray clouds that promised snow. It was silent upstairs. Lassie slept beside the furnace. I could see the dying embers of the last remains of coal. I knew I had better shovel some new chunks of the black stuff into the furnace if I had any hopes of being warm that night.

I got Grampa's leather glove and opened the cast-iron door. The coal bin was in the far corner of the room. The shovel was the same one I used to sit on and slide down the hill. *No wonder my butt is always black,* I thought.

After throwing a few good shovelfuls into the furnace, I decided to go upstairs. The steps creaked beneath my feet. Luckily, the bolt was off the door, so I could get in.

Mother was slumped in the chair, staring out the window, one cheek all swollen and red. She said, without looking at me, "He's gone back to Cleveland to look for work. Your dad's staying with his mother because it's too hard for him to travel back and forth to Avon." I ran to her side and wrapped my arms around her as far as they could reach. I forced the picture of her red cheek out of my mind. I didn't ask because I was afraid of the answer.

I nodded, holding onto this spark of hope offered by Mother. *It makes sense,* I told myself. Then another little voice whispered in my mind: *Except, what about Billy's dad? He drives back and forth to work and doesn't have to stay away for a long time.* I hugged my mom and went into the bathroom to sort things out.

My dad's words to me kept playing over and over in my head: *"What did you do today to earn the ground you're standing on?" How about the ground belongs to my Grampa, and he loves me?* I answered my dad's words. What a stupid question to ask a kid. Why couldn't my dad have just given me a hug? *What a dumb dad. I just can't wait till I grow up. I'll show 'em all how to be a real family. Why, he's probably too much work even for the Blessed Mother to fix.*

Then, in my head, I screamed, *He is a mean fucking bastard and I hate his guts! I hope he dies and goes straight down to hell forever!*

The tears wanted to come, but I refused to cry now or ever again.

CHAPTER SEVEN

The First Snow, 1952

"May the wind be always at your back and the lord hold you in the palm of his hand, till we meet again..."

-- An Old Gaelic Blessing

The days grew colder, and one day melted into the next, and one season passed into another...

I was in the sixth grade and had become a little more forgiving of my dad. I don't know why, except that I think it just took too much energy to keep my hate for him alive. I felt better keeping my dream alive.

It had been two years since I'd seen my father. I continued to pray to the Blessed Mother to make him come home so I could have a real family just like the other kids. I also told her I was sorry for thinking she could not fix him. I knew in my heart she could fix anything.

We got our first snow that year just before Thanksgiving. I woke up during the night, freezing and teeth chattering.

"Mother! Wake up! It's so cold in h-h-here I can't m-m-move!"

"Rub your feet together. Maybe that will help," she mumbled, and pulled the threadbare army blanket over her head. Tommy and Donna could not be seen in their beds, but the telltale lumps under their covers were proof they were there.

I threw back the blanket from my side of the bed and headed toward the kitchen. The floor was like ice where my bare feet touched it. I went into the kitchen closet and started pulling coats no one ever wore off the hangers. I put three winter coats on our bed, one being Aunt Leona's lamb's wool jacket. I stuck my arms in the sleeves and curled up next to Mother. The wind howled and the silent snow piled up as we slept, finally warm.

In the morning, we woke up to a winter wonderland. The radio said that all schools were closed. I sat on the chair in the living room, looking at the ice that had formed on the inside of the window.

Mother came over to me with a little cloth pouch in her hand, remarking, "Just look at the beautiful painting Jack Frost did for us."

We sat together, and I created pictures in my mind from the frosted shapes on the window. She finally handed me the pouch. "Take this cloth with salt in it and rub it on the window to get the ice off."

I rubbed the little pouch on the iced window and watched the scenes melt away. The snow was falling steadily, big flakes swirling in the wind. Lassie lay in front of the old heat register, trying to keep warm.

Finally I had watched the snow long enough; the day now beckoned.

I dressed quickly, then found my red snow pants with the blue suspenders. Black rubber boots came next, because if your sweater and jacket went on first, you couldn't bend over far enough to get your boots on. Finally, I pulled on a pair of my sister's gloves, the finger pockets extending off the ends of my fingers like wet noodles.

Grampa stepped in the house, shaking off the snow from his winter Parka. "It's a cold one out there. You won't be out long, little Maureen. Why, poor old Henry froze to the fence this morning, hanging on by one leg." He pulled out his red polka-dot handkerchief, wiped his nose, and did an imitation of the rooster balancing on one leg. He chuckled at his wit before disappearing into his side of the house.

As I stepped out of the house, the wind caught the door and almost tore it off its hinges. I pulled my scarf up over my nose and slowly trudged through the snow. Halfway down the driveway, I spotted Billy with his sled heading for the hill beside our house.

He waved his arms in the air, and we both raced to meet at the hill. We were filled with so much excitement about the first good sledding day of the season that we never felt the cold.

The wind blew, freezing the snow on our scarves and mittens in little round pill balls. Lassie's tail and the fur under her stomach gathered big clumps of snow as she tried to follow us up and down the hill.

I didn't have a sled, but Grampa's old coal shovel worked quite nicely. I sat on the blade with the handle between my legs and flew down the hill, my scarf trailing in the wind. Billy followed close behind on his "American Red Flyer." The tough part was climbing back up the hill. We gladly accepted the challenge, our cheeks bright red from the icy wind.

"Maureen, let's go see if the pond's froze." Billy's muffled voice emerged from beneath his dark green scarf. His brown eyes looked at me through the small space between the scarf and stocking cap.

We stood at the top of the hill, with the trails of Billy's sled and my shovel grooved in the deep snow below us. The snow plow had not been through yet, and sweeping drifts lay from our hill and across the street clear over to the pond. The branches of the pine trees hung heavy with sculpted mounds of snow that glistened in the bright sun.

I didn't have to think twice. "Let's go, Billy!"

We headed across Stoney Ridge, leaving a trail of footprints. The maples, now barren of any leaves, bowed gray frozen branches to the wind. The snow was so deep, we could scarcely see where the ground stopped and the pond began.

"Lookie here, Maureen, it's frozen." Billy stood on a patch of ice he'd uncovered. We looked at each other as if we had discovered gold.

By now, Kathie Bauers and Sandra Hemmer had stopped throwing snowballs, and came to join in our excitement.

"Let's get shovels and clear the pond so we can skate," said Kathie. She was a new kid. I really didn't know her, but I liked her, even if she did wear thick glasses. Sandra was big for her age, and I figured that if the ice held her, we'd all be safe.

We all decided to head home for lunch and dry clothes, get shovels, and meet back at the pond. So our plan was in place. Lassie and I, covered in frozen snow, went in through the basement and found a nice warm place in front of the old coal furnace. I sat on the cement floor and pulled off one snow-filled boot at a time, then worked my way up until my frozen clothes lay in a heap beside the furnace. I flew up the steps in my dungarees and red cardigan.

Mother turned from the stove as I banged through the kitchen door. "Just look at your face!" she exclaimed. "You've been outside for hours! Sit down here and have some lunch." She poured me a bowl of steaming potato soup and handed me a slice of freshly baked bread, still warm from the oven. On the table, a bottle of Dairymen's Milk sat, still half-frozen, cream oozing through the cardboard lid.

I scooped my soup from the edge of the bowl and blew it gently before sipping. "You sure are the best cooker, Mother."

Mother took the lid off the bottle of milk and poured some into my soup. "Try this. It'll cool your soup off so you can eat it."

This was one of those rare moments when I felt like a queen in her castle -- broken-down castle that it was. The kitchen was warm and smelled delicious. I sat rubbing my toes together and enjoyed my lunch. I looked out the window at the flurry of kids sledding down the hill and throwing snowballs. Finished with my soup, I pushed back from the table and hurried downstairs to dress and join them.

My snow clothes were still damp, but I put them on anyway. Time was a wastin', and the pond was frozen.

Tommy's old hockey skates hung on a nail next to the washtubs. Because they were five sizes too big for me, I stuffed the toes with newspaper and headed back across Stoney Ridge for Bauers's Pond. By now, the big kids had arrived and cleared off the snow.

Billy came flying past me, skating more on his ankles than the blades. "Maureen, get your skates on! The ice is great!"

A pile of boots lay at the edge of the ice where the kids had changed into their skates. I sat down and threw my boots in with theirs, and laced up the size-10 hockey skates.

Dick and Don skated over to me. Don said, "Hey, Richards, watch what you're doing and don't get any snow on my boots. What do you think you're doing with those big old skates on, anyways?" They skated away, laughing at the looks of me.

Well, that does it, I thought, and proceeded to stuff their boots with ice and snow.

I took off across the ice, feeling very satisfied with myself. We played ice hockey and tag late into the afternoon. The temperature dropped and the big kids built a bonfire to keep warm. The blizzard had passed, and the temperature was dropping. The sky filled with some gray clouds, allowing the sun to peak through and slowly sink in the blazing horizon.

"Look, Billy," I pointed at the sky.

He nodded solemnly.

"When the sky looks like that, it means Santa Claus is baking."

"I hope it means my mom's baking," he replied, then added, "I better go home, I'm freezin'." With that he stood, covered in frozen snow, teeth chattering. "Meet ya here tomorrow if there's no school, Maureen." Then, turning his head, he sunk it down into his shoulders as far as it would go to keep the chill off, and trudged through the snow for home.

I looked back at the now-deserted pond and decided to take a couple of turns around the ice. It was as if I was flying effortlessly, the only noise the hissing sound of my blades cutting into the ice. Before I knew it, it was dark and snowing again. Snowflakes swirled and blew around me as I changed back into my boots and walked across Stoney Ridge.

The soft golden glow of a single light from our kitchen showed through the frosted front window and glistened on the snow. Shadows from the ice-coated maple branches danced on the drifts.

A chill ran up my spine, and suddenly I was very cold. Maybe, just maybe, my dad would be home to stay when I opened the door. Deep down, I knew I was just playing the "What if" game again. Still, every time I opened the door, I thought, *This could be the time my life will change.*

CHAPTER EIGHT
Christmas 1955

"And in the east, shown a star, one shining Star..."

-- Christmas Gospel

Winter passed, and then another and yet another. Aunt Dora had moved to Florida with her family, and talked my grandfather into moving there also, as the climate would be better for Gramma.

The days grew shorter as Thanksgiving came and went. Mother, Donna, Tommy, and I shared noodle soup and stewed chicken, grateful for something warm to eat, and grateful for each other.

Finally, it was the last day of school before Christmas vacation. The class was seated and waited for Sister Mary Adorika to speak.

"Attention, children," she began as she tapped the little silver bell on her desk so that we would give her our complete and undivided attention. "We're going to line up and go over to church for choir practice for Christmas."

We obligingly lined up, Kathie Bauers behind me. Her long pigtails hung over the front of her shoulders. Her small green eyes looked through thick glasses into mine as she whispered, "Let's sit together, okay?"

The excitement of the birth of Jesus filled the air. We held hands as we walked across the schoolyard, the wind blowing unmercifully against our bare legs. Girls were not allowed to wear pants or leggings to school because the Blessed Mother always wore a gown. But, then again, she didn't grow up in Ohio.

I whispered to my partner, "Wish we could wear snow leggings to school, Kathie. I'm freezing."

"Me, too," she said.

I whispered again. "Just hang on and try not to slip, or we'll both go down."

We skated in our boots across the frozen snow, two friends together, laughing.

"I want complete and utter silence," Sister announced as we paused at the vestibule of the church. Her face was stark white and expressionless. She had a reputation for being downright cruel, and no one ever tested it.

It took a few minutes, as always, for my eyes to get used to the dimly lit church. The air was thick with the scent of the fresh-cut pine draped from one pew to the next, all the way up to the altar. The deep burgundy carpet running up the center aisle led to a Nativity scene surrounded by huge poinsettia plants.

Sister spoke just above a whisper, showing reverence to this holy of all holy places during this, the most celebrated holy day of the church. "Children, we'll sit in the first row in front of the infant Jesus's crib. On the bench, you'll find paper and pencil. You are to write one

Christmas wish and put it in the manger with Baby Jesus."

We filed down the center aisle, boots rattling as we went, and took our places in the front row. I stared at the Wise Men, decorated in brilliant robes, bearing their gifts for Baby Jesus. The statue of the Blessed Mother seemed even more radiant than usual. Her beautiful blue gown and veil surrounded her soft delicate features. I wanted to reach out and touch it. Kathie poked me.

"Aren't you going to write something?" she whispered.

All I could do was nod. I could feel my eyes filling with tears, which then spilled over as I wrote:

Dear Jesus,

Me and your mom, the Blessed Mother, are really good friends. I talk to her all the time at my Butternut Tree. I love you. Thank you for all the wonderful blessings you have given me, like Billy and my new friend Kathie.

There is only one thing I really need. You've given me everything, except... please, dear Jesus, give me my dad back. I want the one my mom talks about that loved her and me, Tommy, Donna, and Ted. Just think of it, Dear Lady. Mother said they used to sing together when they were drying the dishes.

All my friends have dads. I guess I don't because I'm so bad and say swear words. If you do this for me, I promise never to say another bad word as long as I live.

Your friend, Maureen

# # #

Wiping my tears off my face, I was grateful for the dimly lit church. A quiet came over me as I sat with my friend

Kathie, our voices echoing all the timeless Christmas carols.

As we were leaving, Sister Mary Medaleva pulled me aside. Sister Mary Adorika was standing by her. I had no idea what I did, but decided it must have been really bad to have these two after me.

Sister Medaleva spoke first.

"What is it, child? You carry a burden that breaks our hearts. Please tell us how we can help."

I looked from one to the other in shock. They were human. They had feelings. They actually cared. Sister Mary Adorika's eyes, which I had thought always looked so cold, had a tender softness in them.

I gathered up my nerve to speak. "I'll tell you, Sister, because I think I see Jesus in your eyes. My dad didn't really get shot in the war. He lives in Cleveland and only comes home when he's drunk. My mother says he was not always like that. He used to be gentle and kind. I prayed he would come back home and love us all again.

Maybe then my mom will not be so sick all the time, and we'll be a real family."

I looked over my shoulder at the center aisle where the families sat. "See the family section? I just want to sit there one time with my whole family together, just one time."

Sister took my chin in both of her wrinkled hands and gently wiped the tears off my face. "Little Maurveen, trust in da Baby Jesus, he lufs you very much. Sister und I vill say special Christmas prayers dat your family is togetder again. Meanvile, come mit us to our kitchen. It's a very colt day, und ve should haf hod chocolade."

The school bell chimed the end of the day. As I followed the Sisters, their black hand-knitted shawls wrapped tightly around their shoulders, they looked so much smaller than in previous years.

Together we entered their modest kitchen, filled with the aroma of fresh-baked *kuchen*.

"Cook, ve haf a guest. Blease pour some hod chocolade."

I had never been inside of the Sisters' quarters, but felt right at home. I stomped the snow from my boots and took them off on the small frayed rug by the door. I knew the Sisters were not allowed to eat in front of anyone except another Sister, so I understood when they did not have coffee with me.

Sister Medaleva patted my back. "I have a feeling everything is going to be just fine. Christmas brings miracles." She disappeared down the hallway.

I looked out the window at the pine trees bending in the wind. The hot chocolate was too rich for me, but I drank it anyway because I didn't want to hurt their feelings. They were trying so hard to help, and I loved them for it. I thanked them, left, and headed for Kathie's.

Her little white house was nestled in the middle of pine trees heavy with snow. Kathie watched out the window as I came up the drive, and she pulled open the door for me. A huge Christmas tree stood all decorated in the corner of the living room. A fire roared in the red-brick fireplace; seven stockings hung from the mantle. Toys were scattered on the floor where Kathie's sisters Julie, Dottie, and Sarah played with their baby brother, Patrick.

"Maureen, what happened to you? I looked around when we came out of the church, and you were gone. Marie Little said you were in trouble with Sister."

"Marie Little always thinks she knows everything that's going on, and when she doesn't know, she just makes stuff up."

"Can you stay for supper and spend the night? It's the first day of vacation tomorrow, so we could stay up late and make popcorn."

"I'll run back home and check on my mom."

Arriving home, I found that Mother was in bed with the covers pulled up over her head. It wasn't even dinnertime, so I knew she must be sick again. I looked around the cold bedroom. Clothes were piled high on the chair in the corner. The gray-painted floor was so dirty, you could see footprints in the dust.

I threw some clothes in a paper bag and ran back over to Kathie's warm and festive home. We had supper, with everyone talking at once about Christmas, then went to Kathie's room to play games and talk. We had just become friends, as she was the new kid this year. I told her the whole story about my dad and my life. We both laughed so hard when I explained how I told the nosy neighbors my dad got shot dead in the war. I then told her about the Sisters being kind to me. We took turns scratching backs and swore we'd be friends forever.

# # #

Come December 24th, we still had no tree at home. So I decided to take matters into my own hands.

The Moore family had a Christmas tree farm just on the other side of the creek. I jumped into my snowsuit, grabbed a saw from the basement, and Lassie and I went on our mission. The creek was frozen solid, and there were patches of old frozen snow here and there throughout the woods. My hands were freezing in the white church gloves I'd had to settle for. The weather was very cold and dry. We had prayed all week for a white Christmas, but our prayers had yet to be answered.

Spotting a small fir tree at the edge of the clearing, I went to work. After cutting it down, I noticed a small bird nest at the top. *Perfect,* I thought. *This makes it even more special.*

The wind was picking up, and heavy gray snow clouds were gathering in the sky. Reaching home, I dragged the little tree in through the front door and stuck it in the corner of our tiny living room.

"Oh my God, Maureen, where did you get the tree?" Mother was out of her robe and dressed for the first time in weeks. "I'll round up some decorations. You are really something, kiddo."

She rummaged through the closet and found an old box filled with silver bulbs, half of them broken. A few clumps of gnarled tinsel clung to the bottom of the box. "Let's turn on the radio and listen to Christmas carols," she suggested.

As Bing Crosby crooned "White Christmas," Mother and I started to decorate our tree. We found one string of frayed lights and added it as the finishing touch. Night fell, and Mother and I sat quietly, staring at our tree.

The screen door slammed on the front porch. Before I could jump out of my chair, the front door flew open and Tommy and Donna stepped in. Donna had on a beautiful red wool coat with matching hat and scarf. Tommy's red wool stocking cap was pulled over his ears. His brown dress slacks looked to be two sizes too small, leaving three inches between the cuffs and shoes. He was tall for his age and really quite handsome.

"Where did you guys get the beautiful clothes?" I asked.

Tommy wiped his nose with his glove and said, "The rich kids brought boxes of clothes to the church while me and the other high school altar boys were practicing for Christmas Mass. Father called me aside when the other kids left, and told me if we needed anything, I could help myself."

He was so excited that he had found a coat for Donna that she had actually put on. I could tell by the look on her face, though, that it wasn't going to stay on. She said, "Tommy, I think this was a friend of mine's that cheers with me in high school. So I know you'll understand when I don't wear it to mass -- or any place else she might be, for that matter."

Tommy's face lost its excitement, but he took it well and made a joke out of it like we all learned to do when something hurt. "Actually, Donna, I think you'd better throw it out." He pointed to the sleeve of the coat. "Look, there's Kelloge snot on the sleeve."

We all howled with laughter. After that, Christmas music from the old Emerson radio filled our little house. Mother sat by the tree in the living room, with all the other lights off. With her hair pulled back from her delicate features, and in the soft glow of the tree, she looked like an angel -- so perfect, so gentle, so beautiful.

"Mother?" I asked. "Are you coming to Midnight Mass with us? Please come. We'll march up the center aisle and sit in the family section, right in the front row, because I said special prayers in church today and even wrote a note to Baby Jesus to bring Dad home. I think he might show up for real if we all go to Mass and sit in the family section."

Everyone exchanged glances, and I felt so stupid for telling them. Mother spoke first. "Well, I think that was a wonderful prayer, and we can all go to church together and sit wherever we please."

As we walked to church, the air was bitter cold and the wind blew unmercifully at our backs. We huddled together, walking up the frozen cindered path past Billy's, the Dunkers', and the Binzes' houses to St. Mary's.

I sniffed at the air. "I sure hope it snows. It smells like snow, don't you think, Tommy?"

"It does smell like snow, runt. Maybe you should write another note to Baby Jesus." He pulled me close and gave me the best Christmas hug ever.

Our excitement grew as we approached the church. Finally, we stood on the steps of St. Mary's.

Donna squeezed my hand.

"Look, Boguidie, it's the Star!"

Gray fluffy clouds sailing across the dark sky parted to reveal a single star. The star was shining brightly through the tall pines and frozen maple branches. We stood in awe as the story of the first Christmas unfolded in our thoughts.

Entering the church, we walked up the center aisle, hand in hand, while the choir sang: "Hark the Herald angels sing, glory to the newborn King..." We sat in the family section, second row, right next to Joycie and Jacob. Joycie had a red wool stocking cap on her head, replacing the big ugly bows of her younger days. Jacob's hair was slicked back, and he looked very serious in his navy-blue suit and brown winter top-coat. I sat glued next to Mother and looked at Tommy on my left, then glanced at my beautiful sister Donna on the other side of Mother. All we needed, I thought, was my dad.

After all, it was Christmas. Maybe he missed us and would just walk right up the aisle any minute now. Or maybe he was just a horse's hinder, and we were a family without him anyway. Maybe we'd always been a family and I just didn't know it. I glanced again at Mother, Tom, and Donna. A quiet peace warmed my heart, body, and soul. *Oh, thank you, Blessed Mother,* I thought. *I get it now. We don't need anyone else. We have each other.* With that, I bowed my head and prayed.

I whispered to Mother, "I'm so glad we got to church early. We not only got the best seats, we get to see everyone come in. See, it's finally happening. We're sitting here in the family section, just like I said we would a long time ago. I made one mistake though. I thought we needed a dad to be a whole family. I was wrong. All we needed was each other."

Mother took out an old lace-trimmed hanky to catch a tear sliding down her cheek. Her lips quivered as she said, "How did you ever get so grown up?" She smoothed my hair from my eyes and gently pulled my face to hers. "Now you just behave yourself if Mrs. Wagner comes in."

"I promise, but it'll be hard...very hard."

Mother cleared her throat and sat back in the pew.

I thought I could do it, too, until the Wagner family strutted up the aisle and perched right in front of us. Dick and Don turned and gave me their usual "snarl." The brim of Mrs. Wagner's very large, green felt hat extended just inches from the end of my nose as I knelt and she sat. I could feel Mother, Tommy, and Donna's eyes on me as they waited to see what I would do.

I turned, very slowly for effect, to level a gaze at the three of them. Mother squinted her eyes at me; Donna shook her head "No"; and Tommy had already covered his mouth in anticipation. I gently tapped Mrs. Wagner on the shoulder and heard a gasp from poor Mother.

"Merry Christmas, Mrs. Wagner. May I tuck the price tag in on your hat? Or are you going for the Minnie Pearl look this holiday?"

She turned quickly as I touched her, then frantically searched the edges of her hat for the price tag that was not there.

I sat back in my bench with my eyes straight ahead. I finally turned to Mother and whispered, "I didn't break my promise. I didn't stick out my tongue."

Donna's face was red; and all I could see of Tommy was the back of his head as he left the church to get some fresh air.

Billy and his family had made their way down the aisle and taken the seat directly behind us, touching each one of us on the shoulder as they found their places.

"Merry Christmas, Merry Christmas, everybody," they said.

Billy's eyes were flashing with excitement. "We opened presents before we came to Mass, Maureen. I got a new pair of hockey skates and a tackle box. Meet me at the pond tomorrow if you can sneak out, it bein' Christmas an' all."

"Hey Billy! We're all sitting in the family section. I got Tommy, Donna, and my mom. My whole family is here."

He waved and mouthed "Merry Christmas" at my family, then leaned forward and whispered in my ear. "I know you wanted that more than anything Maureen, and I'm glad you got 'em all here." He shook my shoulder, then sat down.

Having regained control of himself, Tommy had returned and was sitting at the end of the row. The church was packed with people, all bundled in their warmest coats of every color.

A few late stragglers searched the already overstuffed pews for seats. I looked up just in time to see my brother stand and help poor old "Gallstones" into his seat. Thick, frizzy gray hair stood out from under a black beanie hat crammed down over her ears. Her thick glasses fogged over as she leaned toward Donna and Mother, clutching her huge handbag. "Now, there's a real gentleman." She wiped her red nose with her hanky. "Merry Christmas, all," she said in her usual raspy voice, grinning widely.

The organ stopped, and a hush fell over the little congregation. Everyone stood and turned to face the back of the church, where the processional had formed. The altar boys, dressed in their black-and-white starched hacek altar clothes, swung the chain-suspended incense lanterns. Smoke swirled to the ceiling and hung there. Mrs. Shumacker struck the organ keys in a verse of "Oh Holy Night," and the processional moved up the aisle to the altar.

I spotted old Crecker, one of the Bindelstiffs from the park, standing by the side entrance. His face was scabby and beet-red from booze and the frigid weather.

Father stretched out his arms and said, "Merry Christmas. The peace of Christ, child, be with you."

Crecker yelled out, "Ah, bullshit! It's all bullshit!" He then turned and stumbled out the door. A gasp echoed through the church, along with muffled chuckles. *Poor Crecker, out in the cold night air by himself,* I thought, and felt so sad for him.

When Mass was over, the church filled with the music of "Silent Night." I held tightly to my sister, brother, and Mother as we inched our way to the huge oak doors. The fresh, bitter-cold air greeted us as we entered the vestibule. In the far corner stood Sister Mary Adorika. She held out one of her arthritic, wrinkled hands, and touched my shoulder before she spoke.

"I see you und your family are all togedder ad mass." She smoothed down my hair and smiled. "Somedimes da Lord vorks in strange vays." Once again she held her head high and looked down her nose at me.

I could not imagine how, years ago, I had thought her eyes were cold. Now, I could only see the love of God shining through them.

She gave me a hug and winked. "Frohe Weihnachen, Merry Christmas," she whispered, and disappeared back into the church.

The light from the tiny church spilled out onto glistening snow as we stepped out into the frigid night air.

"It's snowing!" we all echoed together.

Large snowflakes continued to fall as people huddled together, chattering about the Christmas snow. With breath frosting in the air, they soon covered their mouths with warm scarves and scurried for home. Tommy made the first snowball, his face and cheeks red from the cold. Snowflakes stuck to his cap and jacket as he threw it at me.

"That's war!" I shouted, "Christmas or not!"

Soon, snowballs flew in all directions as Billy and his brothers joined in the fun.

I glanced down at Billy's hands. "Where are your gloves?"

"Gloves are for sissies." His red frozen fingers clutched one last snowball. He flung it, hitting Dick Wagner smack in back of the head. He quickly stuck his hands in his pockets before Dick could turn to see who threw it.

"That one was for you, Maureen," my best friend said. "Merry Christmas!"

CHAPTER NINE

Honoring the Promise, 1986

"Oh my God, Daniel, it's still here!" I ran down the path to the old tree that hung over the creek, with my son at my heels.

The weather was warm for May in Ohio, the grass a lush green. The woods -- thick with tall trees -- surrounded the gray, twisted remains of Grampa's apple orchard.

This is where I grew up. This place is part of my soul. This is the old homestead I was raised on, I thought as I felt a quiet, almost holy, calm descend upon me.

The soft sound of trickling water, broken only by a robin singing, welcomed me home. I embraced my Butternut Tree like a long-lost friend, a comrade who had shared my daily battle of growing up in this self-righteous community. My tree, my comrade, had shared my deepest thoughts, my fears, and my dreams for many years of my young life. It had survived, and so had I.

For so many years, I had thought that I hated this place. But now the realization came crashing down on me how deeply I loved it.

"It's here," I choked out through my sobs to my son, standing quietly on the path above the water's edge. "It's still here, after all this time."

I held the tree in my arms and looked through those old branches reaching up to the bright blue sky, tears streaming down my face. I listened to the comforting sounds of the world I had loved so many years ago. It still held its magic, and quieted me now as it did then.

"It's so beautiful," I whispered.

"Mom, are you okay?" My son's voice was filled with emotion. He knew my heart, and was wise beyond his years.

"I can't remember when I've ever been better, Daniel," I laughed through my tears. "I know it's hard to believe to look at me."

My son wrapped his arms around me. He held me close and said, "It's your turn to cry in my arms, Mom." And I did as I stood under my Butternut Tree, realizing I had fulfilled the promise I had made so many years ago on this very spot where I stood with my youngest son.

I had lost track of the time. "Daniel Jon, what time is it? We need to get to the airport to pick up your dad, Kathie, and Chas."

He looked at his watch. "It's time to go, Mom; their plane lands at four o'clock. Do you still remember any shortcuts to Cleveland Hopkins Airport? We may get stuck in rush hour."

I had to laugh and said, "This is not California, sweetheart, so traffic is nowhere near the gridlock we're used to. We can take some back roads to save time. There is so much I want to show you on some of these old back roads I traveled as a kid."

We walked up the overgrown path towards the old farm house I grew up in. "So, Mom, are you going to show me where you and Dad used to park after school?"

"Oh yes, I'll be sure and do that, honey. Did I ever tell you about the time we were making out and..."

Daniel put his fingers in his ears as he always did when he did not want to hear what I was going to say, and did the "La la la" chant.

"Just kidding, Mom," he added when he saw that I was going to continue on the dreaded subject of his mother and father "making out." I learned quickly that the fastest way to stop our teenage children when they had questions about their parents' sex life was to call their bluff and act like I was really going to tell them and leave nothing out.

"We better hurry back to the car, Daniel. I told Aunt Donna we'd meet her at the hospital before we go into Grandma's room."

We got into the rental car, and I sat with my hands on the steering wheel, looking at the old, empty house I grew up in. It felt like it had died, and in a way, it had.

"Mom, are you okay to drive? I can get us to the airport. Just tell me when to turn. I promise not to speed."

"No, I'm fine. I just wish my mom would walk out that front door." I choked back the tears that wanted to come. "She did not know me the last time I saw her. I'm not sure Tommy was right to have her put on life support."

"What a horrible decision for a son to have to make, Mom. I would have done the same thing unless I knew you did not want that."

Backing out of the driveway, I turned onto Stoney Ridge. "Look there, Daniel Jon, Bauers's Pond." Houses surrounded my old fishing hole. The cattails and red-winged blackbirds had disappeared. Bauerdale Court entered Stoney Ridge at the top of the hill. I put on my turn signal just before passing it.

"Let's stop at Aunt Donna's house just for a minute." My sister and her husband, Al, had built their home shortly after they were married. Life was good for a while, then Al got sick and died. Donna, being Donna, managed to keep her home and raise their three children by herself. She had never ceased to amaze me as a child; so it came as no surprise that she could do the impossible on such a limited income.

Tommy never married. Mother was living with him at the time that I married my high school sweetheart Chuck and moved to California.

"I love Auntie's house, Mom. Look how big the trees have grown." As we stepped out of the car, my sister opened her front door. I ran into her arms, clinging to her like a child again. We held to each other, sobbing. Mother was dying. Daniel Jon wrapped his arms around us until we were able to speak. I wiped the tears from my sister's still-beautiful face as she gently returned the favor.

"Daniel Jon, just look how tall you are," she said. "Congratulations on getting into medical school."

"Thanks, Auntie, got any pie?"

I looked at my watch. "Oh my God, we have to get to the airport to pick up the rest of the family!"

Walking us to the car, Donna said, "I'll meet you at the hospital in an hour. Be careful driving."

We made our way to the airport with Daniel Jon reading the road signs from the passenger seat. "These roads have changed so much. My beautiful fields of birds and flowers are all houses now. It's so sad."

"Mom, you need to write a book."

I had often thought of writing about my life -- but now I knew it was something I felt compelled to do.

We circled in front of the United Airlines baggage claim a few times before seeing the rest of my family waiting at the curb for us. "There they are, Mom!"

I pulled the car to a stop right in front of where they stood. My oldest son, Chas, left his suitcase on the curb and ran over to my side of the car and opened the door for me. I stepped out and into his arms. "Mom, are you all right? How is Grandma?"

I looked up into his dark brown-eyes and said, "I'm fine now."

My husband Chuck walked around to my side of the car and put his arms around my son and me, pulling me close to him. His hug meant the same as it always had throughout the thirty-five years of our marriage: Unconditional love. Kathie, flanking me on the other side, searched my face for any clue as to what I was feeling. She was at a loss for words and just hugged me and whispered, "Love you, Mom."

Daniel Jon collected their abandoned luggage from the curb and put it into the trunk of the car. An airport policeman was frantically waving his arm and blowing the silver whistle that was clenched between his teeth at us. Chuck slid into the driver's seat as Daniel Jon, Kathie, and I jumped into the back seat of the spacious town car. Chas sat next to his father in the front seat. My six-foot-five-inch son had long since claimed his place in every car we rode in, never contested by his mom, brother, or sister.

"Maureen, I don't even recognize this place, honey; I hope you know where to turn." I sat snuggled in between Daniel Jon and Kathie. I closed my eyes and said a silent prayer. *This is all I need to get through this, Blessed Mother. Thank you for being my mother and my friend for all these years.*

Chuck slowed the car, waiting for directions. "Look at the map, it's on the seat somewhere," I replied. Chas leaned forward and pulled the wrinkled paper out from under him.

"Lots of luck reading it now, Dad," was Kathie's quick retort. Now I felt a much-needed sense of normalcy. Had she passed up a chance to take a shot at one of her brothers, it would have sent me into a state of shock. Chuck kept looking at me in the rearview mirror. The gray at his temples accented his bright blue eyes. I caught his eye and said, "Love you," and I did so with all my heart.

Chas turned in his seat to face me. "Mom, I wish I could have flown out with you and Daniel. I had to fly to Phoenix to meet with my boss at the last minute."

"I know, honey. Dad told me you called. I think it was better that you could all come at the same time. Actually, by the time Daniel and I got to the hospital, it was past visiting hours, and the nurse on duty at the intensive care unit would not let us in. It was almost midnight, so I clamped my hand across Daniel's mouth before he got us both thrown in jail, and we went directly to the motel down the street."

"Mom, I hardly think we would have gotten thrown in jail for just trying to see Grandma," Daniel retorted in self-defense.

"I know, sweetheart, but your face was turning purple and your voice was escalating far above a 'whisper'."

"Good thing Dad wasn't there, Mom; he would be in jail for sure," Kathie chimed in.

Chuck just continued driving, shaking his head in agreement.

"OK, Mom, but let me tell them about the 'motel from hell'. We get to this motel that Mom said was closest to the hospital and checked in. Of course, the night clerk looked like something out of the movie 'Deliverance'. There he is, grinning from ear to ear at Mom, with the most disgusting mouth full of rotten teeth. I took one look at Mom and knew she'd had it. I said nothing and got her to our room. I went into the bathroom to take a shower, only to find a dirty crumpled-up washcloth sitting on the tub. Mom must have seen it too because she was sleeping on top of the bed in her clothes."

There was silence in the car until Kathie said, "Just tell me we are not staying there before I open the car door and make a run for it." We all howled at her wit, which, for a few minutes at least, broke the heartache we all were feeling.

We pulled into the hospital parking lot and made our way to my mother's room.

Donna and Tommy were standing at the side of her bed. I walked to the other side, with my family close behind.

She scarcely had a wrinkle on her face. I felt the tears sliding down my face. I kissed her cheek and she turned her head, her dark-brown eyes looking directly into mine, and said in a soft whisper that only I could hear, "That crazy Gracie. She said she knew those thugs at the dance hall. It's just a darn good thing we got away." As she finished speaking, her eyes held a look of terror that I had never seen before.

Daniel was crying so hard that I went over to him and took him into my arms. "Mom, looking at the three of you with Grandma, I see three children crying for their mother, and it breaks my heart." He was exactly right. When it comes to your mother, no matter how old you are, the child inside lives forever.

Donna and Tommy walked to the end of Mother's bed to hug the rest of my family and me. It had been years since they had seen us all together. I usually made one trip a year back to Ohio to see my family, and Billy too, of course.

Mother died that night in her sleep. No arrangements had been made as yet, so the following afternoon I found myself walking up the same sidewalk I knew so well to the parish house. Chuck rang the doorbell and a young priest opened the door.

"You must be Mr. and Mrs. Kostalnick, please come in." We followed him into his office and watched him sit down behind the same desk in front of which I had stood so many years ago. The beautiful cherry wood walls had only gotten more beautiful with time.

"I understand that you attended St. Mary's school, Mrs. Kostalnick; please have a seat," he said, motioning to the chairs in front of his desk. Chuck pulled my chair out for me and then sat down in the chair next to me.

"Yes I did, Father, many years ago. My Grandfather DeChant carried the bricks to build the foundation when he was a boy. I was also baptized and made my first holy communion here at St. Mary's. And Chuck and I were married here in 1960." The old days came flooding back and so did the tears. Except this time I was not alone. I had my Chuck and three beautiful grown children that comprised the family I had always prayed for.

"You and your family have a wonderful history here at St. Mary's, and I can assure you that whatever you need I will make sure it is taken care of."

I had to bite my tongue to keep from laughing out loud. A little voice in my head said, *"If you only knew, Father."*

Chuck took out his checkbook and wrote out two checks. "Here, Father, this check will take care of the gravesite and any other expenses." He held up the second check and said, "This one is a donation given in the name of Laura Dorothy DeChant Richards, Maureen's mother and our children's beloved grandmother."

Father looked at both checks and said, "Oh my, this is quite a sizable donation."

Taking my hand as we stood up to leave, Chuck said, "Perhaps the next time we visit we will see a stained-glass window in the vestibule in her honor."

Father walked us to the door and said, "What a wonderful idea, Mr. Kostalnick. Rest assured I will see to that."

Once outside, I turned into my husband's arms and said, "You are truly amazing. Thank you for healing my heart."

Holding me close, he whispered, "I can't stand to see you hurting. I just want to be done with this and take you and the kids back home."

Two days later my family and I followed the small procession carrying my mother's casket into St. Mary's Church. We were seated in the coveted "family section" I had yearned to sit in as a child. I had just sat down when I felt someone rub my back. I turned to see Billy and his wife, Jeanie. "Sorry about your mom, Maureen." My family stood and met my childhood hero;

then we sat down as Father began the service.

There were so many things I wanted to say to honor her. But where would I start?

On the left of the altar stood the statue of the Blessed Mother. My thoughts strayed back to Mother kneeling in front of her and praying. What had happened to her? I knew in my heart that she lived with a horrible nightmare that would not go away no matter how hard she prayed. Mother's haunting words before she died echoed in my head. I knew what I had to do. I only hoped I could find some answers.

The priest stood at the center of the altar and turned to face us. He stretched out his arms and said, "Peace be with you."

Mother's casket was within arm's reach of the outside seat where I sat. I reached over and placed my hand on the top of it as my family and I stood. We held hands in the traditional manner and replied, "And also with you."

My hand gently rubbed the simple pine box. "I know you will stay with me through Eternity, Mother," I whispered.

The mass ended and we followed the tiny procession back to the graveyard. The gravestones stood with the names carved deep into the marble. The smell of fresh-cut grass hung in the air. We walked on the grass, which was still wet from the rain the night before.

"Look, Mom, is that Grandma and Grandpa DeChant's grave?" Kathie stopped next to Mother's gravesite and pointed to the two side-by-side insignificant gray stones.

I read the names aloud. "Theodore James DeChant, Lovina Dorothy Gerhardt DeChant. Yes, that's right, honey, my grandparents and your great-grandparents."

Clearing his throat, Father delivered the final blessing of the grave. When he was finished, he again offered his condolences and left my family and me standing around Mother's grave. Chas handed me the bouquet of roses he had been holding for me. "Thanks, honey." I handed a single rose to be placed on Mother's casket to each member of our small family. I held the last rose. Silent tears trickled down our cheeks.

Kathie walked up to Mother's casket and gently placed her rose on the top, then stood back and lowered her head in prayer for her grandmother. The pride swelled in my chest, just looking at the woman she had grown into. As always, modeling for her younger brothers what to do in moments like this.

Chas followed in his sister's footsteps. The wind gently blew his sandy blond hair. He stood so tall, all six-foot-five of him. My oldest son, so handsome, so successful; and I felt so proud of the man he'd become. Then Daniel Jon took his rose to give to his grandmother, with my Chuck right on his heels. He placed the rose and turned and sobbed in his dad's arms.

The emotions ran so deep for each one of us. I held my rose and walked up to my mother for the last time. After laying it on the pine box, I stepped back and made a final promise to her. "You suffered your whole life with an unspeakable hurt, Mother. A hurt I think perhaps too hideous for your gentle heart to accept. If I am wrong, I will bury this fear with you, Mother. If I am right, there will be hell to pay for whomever was responsible."

We stood together as a family, and honored my mother. Presently, I turned to my sister Donna, and the two of us led my family from the cemetery. We walked silently together. Then I realized that the next thing after a funeral was to feed everyone.

"Donna, can we just go to that new little restaurant on the corner of Detroit and Stoney Ridge for breakfast?" I offered. She stuffed her Kleenex into her jacket and slid her arm under mine.

"Good idea. They have really good pancakes, and I know how you get when you need food."

Following closely behind us, Chuck and the kids broke into laughter. I turned on my heel to face them and retaliated with "What?" We were all glad to put the anguish aside and find some sense of normal.

Kathie put her arm around my sister and said, "Oh my God, Auntie, you have to know when Mom is hungry you have to feed her or feel her wrath!"

Donna hugged me and replied, "Oh, I could tell you stories about this one and her hamburgers, that's for sure. We just never figured out where it all goes. Look at her -- she's still a stick!"

Sitting in the family-style restaurant, I sipped my coffee, unable to eat, getting my thoughts together for what I was about to share with my family. Finally, I spoke. "Donna, you know the story Mother would tell us about her and her friend Gracie going to the dance hall? When I leaned over to kiss her in the hospital, she whispered, 'That crazy Gracie. She said she knew those thugs at the dance hall. It's just a darn good thing we got away.'"

I continued, "I am not leaving Ohio until I find out what the hell happened to her." I sat my coffee cup down, knowing my family would protest.

"What, Mom? You are not flying back home with us?" Chas was trying to understand what was going on. Chuck sat shaking his head, obviously still angry at my decision, and the knock-down drag-out we'd had the night before about it when I first told him of my decision.

"I know, guys. I am not happy about it either, to say the least. But I need to find some answers if there are any."

Looking at my sister, I said, "I suspect they did not get away. If indeed they did not, that would explain the whispering and the discrimination from all the good Catholics in town."

Then Kathie spoke. "Whatever you need to do, Mom, you know you have our support; we just don't like leaving you here."

"I need time with Donna and Tommy anyhow, so I'll just stay a couple of days and then fly home."

With that, I said goodbye to my family in the parking lot of the restaurant, feeling relieved that I could do what I needed to do on my own. I had always felt that I somehow needed to protect them from the pain of my growing years and what I considered the 'bullshit'.

CHAPTER TEN

Truth, Outrage, and Peace

"...And the truth shall set you free."
-- John 8:32

The light spring rain spattered on the windshield. I glanced at the dashboard, found the wiper button, and pushed it. The rhythmic beat of the wipers began to pound in my ears and seemed to distract me from my thoughts. Deciding I needed quiet, I pushed the button again to turn them off. Now, hearing only the peaceful raindrops on the convertible top, I took a deep breath and said out loud, "That's better." I searched the leather cushioned armrest for the window controls, and lowered the window just enough to hear the wind whistling. "Okay, now I can think," I whispered in an effort to comfort myself.

Mother's last words played over and over in my mind: *"That crazy Gracie. She said she knew those thugs at the dance hall. It's just a darn good thing we got away."*

The unfounded prejudice I had grown up with was beginning to make sense. *What if the town knew something my brothers, my sister, and I did not?* I thought. *Or maybe I'm going off the deep end and should just get on an airplane and go home.*

The latter was just a fleeting thought, however, for I knew I had to find out the truth. If there was no evidence to be found that Mother had not escaped from the men that night, I promised myself that I would bury my torment with my mother and get on with my life.

By the time I pulled into my sister's driveway, the rain had almost stopped. The sun managed to slice between fluffy gray clouds, as I stepped out of the car. A perfectly shaped rainbow graced the sky directly behind Donna's house. I stood staring at the sky.

I'm sure Donna must have seen me get out of the car and wondered what I was gawking at. In a moment, Donna was at my side looking at the heavenly rainbow-streaked sky. "Mother is at peace, Sis," she said. "It's her only way of letting us know."

Turning to Donna, I said, "But I am not at peace. You and I know in our hearts that she did *not* get away -- and I will get to the bottom of this."

We walked together up my sister's sidewalk and into her house. I slipped out of my shoes and left them at the door. A small cream-colored couch sat at one end of the living room, with a soft blue cotton blanket draped over one arm. Shiny hardwood floors led into the immaculate kitchen.

"Sit down, Boguidie, we need tea." I sat on the couch as Donna tucked the blanket around my back. The thought struck me that she had no one to wrap a blanket around her back, and never had for that matter. I shuddered to think of what my life would have been like without her, and said, "Have I ever told you Thank You and how glad I am you're my sister?"

Hugging me, she said, "Me, too."

In a few moments the familiar whistle of her teapot rang out from the cozy kitchen. I shed my blanket to retrieve the noisy pot from the burner. Donna came out from her bedroom just as I was filling our cups.

"Maureen, I never intended to show you this, but know you will never rest until you know the truth. You were right when you said I knew in my heart Mother did not get away. I went to the Cuyahoga County Courthouse two years ago, and found this."

So saying, she opened a newspaper on the kitchen table. *THE CLEVELAND PLAIN DEALER* was dated January 29, 1928. I stared at the bold headlines and read the accompanying article in shock. The article read:

MOBSTERS SENTENCED IN RAPE TRIAL

Johnny Deligeo, known leader of Cosa Nostra in the Cleveland area, and Eddie Jolani were sentenced to one year in prison today for the rape of Grace Webster and Laura DeChant. Both girls are eighteen years old and were abducted from the Columbia Dance Hall.

Feeling a rage I had never experienced before, I looked up at my sister. "What the fuck? You *knew* this and you didn't tell me?" I screamed.

"I was just trying to save you from the pain I felt when I read it, Boguidie."

Grabbing the newspaper, I flew out the door, jumped into my car, and raced off. The stop sign at the end of the street was in front of me before I could stop. My mind was racing. *What the hell have I just found out?* Fire sirens screamed. I pulled to the side of the road and waited for the fire truck to pass. There was no fire truck; the sirens had been screaming in my mind. When the "sirens" stopped, I turned the car around and headed back to Donna's house. *I need to tell her how sorry I am for reacting that way. What an idiot! How could I do that to her?*

The house was locked. I pulled on the door and pounded. "Donna, please open the door!" I sobbed. She was not there. Where had she gone? How was it that I had not passed her leaving as I was returning to her house? Bauerdale was a dead-end street with no other outlet. Maybe she had gone for a walk. Yes, that was it.

I ran around to the back of the house and toward the creek. Tall, wet grass soaked my slacks. "Donna, Donna, I'm sorry! Please, where are you?" I had to slow my pace as I crossed the football field behind her house. Avon High School, where Chuck and I had met. *Oh my God, where has the time gone?*

The wind caught the treetops at the creek, sending pink and white petals from the Dogwoods swirling to the ground. I sat on the bank and watched the muddy water race, not caring about the wet ground or the dirt on my pants.

Donna is fine, I'm fine, all of this will pass, I soothed myself, trying to get a grip and a plan in place. *I need to find the men who ruined my mother's life before I leave here.* A chill ran through me as I walked back to my car. I tried one more time to see if Donna had returned, by looking through her kitchen window. *Donna knows where my hotel is,* I thought. *She might even be there waiting for me, and I need a hot bath.*

Donna was not at my hotel, and there was only message awaiting me, from Chuck. I pushed the message button, and just the sound of his voice calmed me down. "Honey, call me just as soon as you get this message. The kids and I are worried sick about you. Sorry I was such an ass. Just come home and I'll hire a private investigator."

I quickly dialed our number but could only get a busy signal. After trying repeatedly and not being able to get through, I called Kathie, only to find she was not home. Daniel Jon and Chas were not answering their phones either. *What the hell is this?* I thought, then reasoned that they had probably all gone out to dinner. Presently, a tub full of hot water and bubbles beckoned me.

After a good long soak, I called room service and ordered a bowl of soup. I sat in my robe, sipping the steaming broth and dipping a buttered dinner roll into it. Exhausted, I slid into the feather bed.

Rays of sunlight poured through the slice of the drape and spilled onto my pillow. I sat straight up, trying to awaken from what I hoped was just a bad dream. There were no messages from Donna or my family. I tried in vain to reach anyone. After dressing and gulping down coffee and a slice of toast from the hotel's Continental breakfast, I formed a plan. Time was wasting and I needed answers.

Driving to the county courthouse, I enlisted the help of an elderly clerk. I read the name "Jerome" on his ID badge. I showed him the old newspaper. "Oh my, this is tragic," he said. "How can I help you?"

"I need to know if these men are still alive...Laura was my mother." I felt my lip quiver but had no time for tears. I was on a mission, a mission to kill these bastards if they were still alive.

"Oh my, how awful," he said.

Can this well-meaning moron say anything else besides "Oh my?" I wondered, biting my lip in the realization that going off on him would not help anything.

"Give me an hour, Miss, and I will look up these names in our court records. Is there a number I can reach you at?"

Pulling out a chair at a nearby table, I sat down. "No, not really. I'm from out of town, so I'll just wait."

He gave me a blank look and said, "There is fresh coffee, just help yourself."

An hour later, Jerome returned with a piece of paper in his hand and sat down across from me.

"Eddie Jolani died in 1935. I have no record of death for Johnny Deligeo. I bet I can find him if he is still alive, though. What is it worth to you?"

I looked at him and thought, *Is this for real?*

"How about five-hundred bucks?" I offered.

Looking at the diamond on my hand, he countered, "How about a grand?"

"Find him within twenty-four hours and it's a deal."

He gave me a smile and said, "Come back here tomorrow, same time, and I will have the information if there is any to be found."

Returning to my car, I drove straight to Donna's. The house looked the same as it had when I had left it the day before. This was getting more and more weird by the moment. After sitting in her driveway for hours, I decided to drive back to Avon Lake and look at our old neighborhood.

The tri-level brick house at 175 Ashwood Drive -- where Chuck and I had lived when we were first married, before our move to California -- looked lived in. A tricycle on the driveway made me miss my children, my babies. They were all grown up now, and once again I had an empty feeling in the pit of my stomach.

Presently I found myself on Stoney Ridge road, and passed my old house. The streetlights had just come on when I recognized Rose Mitock's house. I pulled into her driveway and sat remembering how she and Nick had been just newly married when I decided to make her my new best friend. I could still see her sweet face looking down at me as the soft summer night pulled me into the past...

"Hi, Rose, wanna come pick violets with me? I'll show you my best patch if you promise not to tell."

She stooped down to meet my stare. "Just how old are you, Miss Maureen? Six? Seven? Going on twenty-seven? Sure, I'd love too, just let me tell Nick..."

The porch light flashed on, bringing me back from my mental trip into the past. I recognized her immediately when she poked her gray-haired head out the door. "Who's in my driveway?" she yelled from her porch.

Oh my God! I thought. *I don't want to give the old girl a stroke.* I slowly opened the door and stepped out, thinking that maybe I should put up my hands because you just don't mess with these old farmers.

"Rose, Rose Mitock? Is that you?"

She took a wary step forward. "Who wants to know? Tell me, and I'll tell you if it's me or not."

I cleared my throat. "Well, I doubt if you remember me, but it's Maureen Richards."

There was silence, then a giggle. "Oh my God! How could I ever forget you? You showed me your favorite violet patch and taught me how to ice skate backwards."

With that, the skinny little lady came running towards me with outstretched arms. We hugged, laughed, and cried all at once. She took my face in her wrinkled hands.

"You little turkey, what are you up to? Come in and have coffee." She opened the front door. Piles of books, paintings, and clothes left only a narrow passage to the kitchen. "Don't mind the mess; I'm in the process of getting rid of junk."

I had heard that she had become a famous artist, painting old barns. I spotted an oil painting of the old red mill by the creek, sitting on an easel. "Oh, Rose, this is just beautiful! I need this! How much?"

Looking over her shoulder at me, she said, "Twice as much for you, little pest. Come sit and let me show you what I've been up to since Tommy and Nick died."

I had heard that her son had gotten killed when he was just in high school, but didn't know about Nick. We sat sipping coffee and catching up on the last forty years.

"About that painting, Rose -- will a hundred dollars do? Did you know that my brother Tommy and his friend Jerry burned that mill down? Yep, they cut school and were back there smoking cigarettes."

She leaned forward in her chair, relishing any little tidbit about the old days.

"Really? That little shit cut the top off my huge pine one Christmas. I sat and watched him and his buddy. I figured it went to a good cause, though, and was thoroughly entertained for at least an hour. Two glasses of wine later I went to bed chuckling."

As I stood to leave, she excused herself and brought out a print of the painting and a map of the old creek and my grandparent's property. "Take this painting from me to you and a copy of my map of the old creek you played on. I call it The Preserve; no one can ever build on it." Then she gave me a wink that only two old friends could understand.

The crickets chirped noisily as Rose walked me to my car. "I'll call you as soon as I get back to California," I said. We hugged a long, wonderful hug, and then I left, vowing to keep in touch with my wonderful childhood friend who had always had time for me.

Back in my car, I headed straight for Donna's. Her living room light cast a warm glow on a figure sitting on her porch. I pulled in and jumped out of the car to meet my sister running down the walkway.

"I am so sorry, Donna, so, so sorry! Please forgive me."

She took hold of my arm to lead me into the house. "No, Boguidie. I handled it poorly. I just can't seem to get past taking care of you and trying to protect you."

I told her about Jerome searching for the one thug that might be still alive.

"You come and get me in the morning; I'm going with you," she said.

I looked at my sister, loving her more than words could express, and missing her so much now that I had made my life in California.

"Come stay with me at the hotel," I offered. "We can have dinner and scratch backs before we go to sleep. Do you think Tommy will come?" I knew he wouldn't, as I don't think he ever got over me leaving him and Mother when I got married.

"No, Maureen. He stays pretty much by himself."

Dinner was perfect. We ate at the old Sample House, which had been turned into a five-star restaurant. Donna ate her salmon baked in parchment, while I had a filet, medium-rare, and two glasses of cabernet.

Leaving the restaurant I said, "You can drive, Sis. I think that wine went straight to my head."

That was all she needed to start singing "Show me the way to go home, I'm tired and I want to go to bed, I had a little drink about an hour ago and it went straight to my head." We harmonized all the way out to the car. It felt so good to laugh and be with my sister.

Awakening the next morning, I found a note on the bathroom mirror from Donna. She'd been sick all night, thought the fish might have been bad, and had gone home. I ordered room service. By the time breakfast came, I had showered and dressed. The hot coffee, poached eggs, and wheat toast made me feel better. My head, however, told me that my second glass of wine had not been a good idea.

It was ten o'clock when I parked the car at the courthouse. Jerome was behind the tall oak counter when I opened the large glass door. "Good morning, ma'am. I did my homework," he said, pulling out a spiral notebook from under the counter. "Let's have a seat here at the table." My heart was pounding as I sat down across from him.

"Johnny Deligeo is in a nursing home in Westlake. Did you bring the money?"

Having withdrawn the cash from the bank right after meeting with him the day before, I handed Jerome the white envelope containing ten one-hundred-dollar bills, and watched him lay the notebook in front of me. I opened the gray notebook cover and read the neatly printed address: Good Shepherd Nursing Home, 3600 Dover Center Road. The place was no more than half an hour away.

"Thank you, Jerome. You certainly came through for me," I said as I stood up and shook his clammy hand.

Calling Donna, I delivered the news, and told her I was going to drive to the nursing home. Then I left the courthouse.

As I stepped outside and made my way back to the car, the sun was bright and the air fresh from the rain the night before. I inhaled deeply, opened the car door, and climbed in. Knowing that I would soon be face to face with one of Mother's rapists, I wished that I hadn't eaten breakfast. Reopening the door, I lost my breakfast on the pavement.

I rolled down the window and let the cool morning air blow on my face as I headed for the nursing home, having no idea what I would do when I got there.

The Good Shepherd Nursing Home, a red-brick one-story building, sat at the end of a long, tree-lined driveway. I parked close to the double-door entrance, got out of the car, and stepped into the building.

A strip of dingy rust-colored carpeting led up to the front desk. A large Hispanic woman gave me a warm smile as I walked in. "Good morning, I'd like to see Johnny Deligeo," I said.

She thumbed the file on her desk and looked up at me. "Oh, how nice. Johnny never gets any visitors. He's in Room 25, on your left and down the hall."

Old people hunched over in wheelchairs lined the walls of the dimly lit corridor. The smell of urine thickened with every step I took along the chipped tile floor. Water-stained ceiling tile blended in with the faded green painted walls. *I think this is a hell of a good place for this bastard,* I thought.

The door of Room 25 was open. The man lying in the bed inside had bone-thin arms resting on stained sheets. Greasy, gray, thin hair and sunken cheeks with a large nose turned to look at me as I stood in the doorway.

"Nurse...please...can I have a drink of water?"

The son-of-a-bitch who had ruined my mother's life thought I was a nurse. Standing there, I felt like the Angel of Death looking at him. I walked over to his bedside. He smelled like he was rotting from the inside out.

"The young woman you raped was my mother!" I managed to choke out in his face. All I received in reply was a blank stare from him.

"Water...please..." he whispered. He reached for my arm and I quickly pulled back so as not to touch the piece of shit.

Retrieving the pitcher of warm, stale water from his nightstand, I filled a dirty plastic glass. Then, holding the glass to his mouth, I poured the water down his throat as I screamed, "Burn in hell, you bastard!" as he started to choke on the water.

The disgusting excuse of an old man who had ruined my childhood and the lives of my brothers and sister lay before me as I continued to scream in his face. "You raped my mother, you fucking bastard! Her name was LAURA! She was just eighteen years old! Because of you and what you did to her, she went to a mental hospital and was never the same again!"

With that, I covered my face with my hands and sobbed. Around me swirled a flurry of activity that had gone completely unnoticed by me until I felt my arms being jerked behind my back by two police officers and handcuffs being snapped onto my wrists.

Donna was there, having driven to the place in the wake of my call, and she held me in her arms. "It's finished now, Boguidie." She rubbed my back, holding me close with her cheek pressed to mine. I felt her warm tears on my face. We were ushered into a private room, where one of the police officers removed the handcuffs from my wrists. He pulled out a chair from a chipped brown ceramic table, and directed me to be seated. A greasy-haired, rotund woman wearing a badge that read "Head Nurse" sat directly across from me. Donna was next to me, and the two police officers stood guarding the door.

The nurse reached out to me and took my hands in hers. "Are you all right?"

Somehow managing to regain my composure, I said, "I am so sorry. I don't know what happened to me in his room. I just saw the reason for my mother's pain lying in that bed, and I went a little nuts. Is he dead?"

She released my hands and said, "No, and I hope he lives long enough to think about what he did. Only God will ever know if he does think about it or not."

The officers came over to the table to talk to the nurse. The older of the two asked, "Are you going to press charges?"

She took a long look at me and said, "No, that won't be necessary. I don't even know who called you."

I watched the younger officer take off his hat and rub his head.

"We got a call from some guy named Jerome. He was worried about having given a woman information about one of your residents. We just dropped in to check it out."

The nurse rubbed my back and said, "I think everything is under control here, officer."

Once outside, Donna and I sat on a bench by the parking lot. "I'm going to puke," I muttered. And I did until there was nothing left inside of me. Then I said, "Get me out of here, Sis."

Returning to my rental car, I opened the door and got in.

Donna said, "Are you okay to drive?"

I nodded "Yes" and looked up at her. "I'm sorry to have put you through this. Am I totally nuts?"

Smoothing back my hair, she said, "Absolutely not. What you did was for our whole family. Remind me never to mess with you," she laughed through her tears. I watched her walk over to her little Ford Fiesta and get in.

"Rest in peace, Mom. I know we are both better now." I whispered as I left the stench of hell behind me.

The sun was warm on my face as I drove to my sister's house. I passed St. Mary's Church and School, with all the memories scattered across the playground I had frequented as a child. I finally understood the prejudice I had grown up with -- and for some reason, it was all okay now.

The aunts and uncles, even my grandparents, probably thought they were protecting us from hurt, the hurt that had impacted and changed each of their own lives.

Four generations of pain caused by the rape of a young innocent girl -- their daughter, their sister, my mother.

Arriving at my sister's house, I pulled in behind her car, where she stood waiting for me. "I need to get back home to my family before they put out a missing persons warrant for me," I said as we walked up her sidewalk and into her living room.

Removing my shoes, I dove onto her couch. "Come sit with me, Sis," I said, and Donna closed the screen door behind her, walked over to me, and sat down. We held each other in silence and wept in each other's arms.

"Come back to California with me. We can take off in my Mini, just the two of us, and go the ocean or the mountains."

She stood and said, "Help me pack."

We both slept most of the way during the flight back to Oakland, California. "Look, Sis, there's our City by the Bay," I pointed out as we neared our destination. We held hands tight and shared the moment without words. When our plane touched down, I whispered yet another prayer to the Blessed Mother. "Thank you, Dear Lady, for seeing me and my family through this horrible ordeal."

Having flown First Class, we were able to exit the plane quickly. We held hands and made our way to the baggage claim.

Pulling up to the curb, where we stood with our suitcases, Chuck yelled "Welcome home!" as he exited the car. "Hi, Donna! So glad you decided to come back with Maureen. The kids are all coming over tonight for dinner."

Chuck loaded our bags in the back of his Escalade, and opened the door for Donna to get in. I had already jumped in the seat beside my Chuck.

California never looked so good. The coastal range was a brilliant emerald green, coated with patches of yellow mustard grass and lavender wildflowers. Orange poppies dotted the roadside, and huge blooming Oleander divided the highway home.

"You expect me to stay in this dump?" echoed Donna's words from the back seat as we pulled into our driveway. Chuck and I cracked up at Donna's wit.

"I know, Sis," I replied. "But look at it this way: As Sister Adorika always said, you're earning a higher place in heaven."

We got settled in and I made a pot of tea for us. Donna came into the kitchen and asked, "Do you mind if I call Dad?"

I looked at her for a long, awkward moment, trying to find the right words. "Of course you can, but why?"

She put her book of phone numbers on the counter beneath the telephone and said, "He hasn't been feeling well, so I just thought I'd check on him."

I put my arm around her, trying to soften what I was about to say. "Really? Oh, I get it -- check on him the way he checked on all of us growing up without him."

I knew Donna had a relationship with him even though he had stuck her and my brothers in an orphanage.

She picked up the phone and I left the room to water my plants outside. When I stepped back into my kitchen, I heard her say, "Well actually I'm in California at Maureen's...Yes, we flew back together after Mother's funeral...Yes, I'll tell her." Looking up and seeing me, she said, "Better yet, you tell her yourself."

And handed me the phone.

Before I had a chance to react, the phone was in my hand. You can only imagine the flood of feelings that consumed me all in a split second.

I took a deep breath. "Hello, Dad. How are you? How's the weather in Cleveland?"

Thank God for the weather, I thought. What else could I have possibly said to the stranger on the other end of the phone? He was very soft-spoken, and I could hear a bit of an Irish accent.

"It's raining, but I don't mind the rain, and I love to hear the wind. It puts me to sleep like a mother's lullaby."

His words sliced into my heart, for, listening to the wind and rain is one of my most favorite things in the world as well. I had barely said "Hello," and I was already at his mercy and hanging onto his every word.

"Well now, Dad, I know how you feel. I grew up listening to the wind and rain blowing through the loose siding of the old house on Stoney Ridge."

There was silence on the phone. I think he was crying.

He finally said, "Stoney Ridge...I wish I could walk that way again...just one more time. I don't like talking about those days. It's very painful. There's not a day that goes by that I don't think of you kids."

I don't know where all the resentment, anger, and bitterness I had lived with all of my life went in that minute. It was just *gone* -- and I was talking to my *dad*. He was very old and sick, and I just felt sorry for him and the fact that we had missed a whole life together. I didn't even know what his favorite food or color was. Something as insignificant as that would have meant the world to me growing up. Anything that would have connected me to him. Anything.

"Maureen, how old are you, and what do you look like?"

"I'm fifty-somethin', Dad, and I'm the picture of my mother, Laura."

Again there was silence, and I knew in my heart that he had paid dearly for his mistakes. My mother loved and forgave him, and so would I to honor her.

"I'll call you again, Dad. It was wonderful to hear your voice," I said.

He answered with words I had long since given up hope of ever hearing from him. "Take care of yourself, Maureen. I love you."

Stunned, I somehow managed to choke out a reply.

"I love you too, Dad. Goodbye."

THE END

ROSE

The rose of my childhood
waits for me...
In her house by my creek
Where we came to be...
Kindred hearts of the spirit
running ever so deep...
With the friendship we knew and
Would always keep...
We lost touch as I grew
but never forgot...
The friend I had
that always took time...
To see what this little girl
had on her mind...
For my Rose was grown
when I was just six...
And took her to my violets
down by the hill...
Overlooking the water
and the "Old Red Mill"...
Now she's painted this picture from
her heart to the print...
Giving the world
only a hint...
Of that "holy ground"
and the peace that we shared...
Through good times and bad
When nobody cared...
Yes, the Rose of my childhood
brings a smile to my face...
That God has given
and time can't erase.

Written October 8, 2009, while flying from my home in California to Ohio to visit Billy, Mayor Jim, Rose, and family.

Old Red Flour Mill, Avon, Ohio
© Rose Mitock

Situated on the Banks of French Creek, with frontage facing Stoney Ridge Road, the "Old Red Flour Mill" was once a thriving industry in the City of Avon, Ohio. Erected in 1830 by James Calhoun, the structure was four stories high, with a sandstone and hard head rock foundation. The function of the Mill was the grinding of wheat, corn, rye, and oats. Wheat was a cash crop and sold for $1.00 a bushel. Bread was the main food at the time. The Mill was approached on Detroit Road from Mills Street, which extended on Stoney Ridge Road. A bridge extended over the creek on Mills Street.

The Mill operated until about 1875, when water power was replaced by steam power. In 1932 the Mill, because of its deteriorating condition, was razed. Later, in 1938, the beams were salvaged. Today nothing remains to mark the Mill's site except for Maureen's memory of it, and the old cable, attached to a large tree branch, that hung over the creek. That part of the creek, just down from The Butternut Tree, was renamed "The Cable," and every kid in town knew its location.

OLD BLUE

WHEN THE NIGHT IS LONG
AND THE DAY'S WORRIES WON'T LEAVE...
I FEEL A COLD NOSE
ON MY PAJAMA SLEEVE...
HOW DOES HE KNOW WHAT'S ON MY MIND?
FOR HE'S JUST A DOG -- WHAT REASON COULD HE
FIND OR EVEN BEGIN TO UNDERSTAND...
ALL OF THE PROBLEMS THAT PLAGUE THIS LAND...
I PAT MY BED FOR HIM TO COME
BUT HIS BONES ARE OLD AND HE CANNOT RUN...
STILL, BLUE TRIES TO JUMP TO SLEEP WITH ME...
WE SEE HOW HARD GROWING OLD CAN BE...
I HEAR HIS SIGH AND FEEL HIS STARE...
HE KNOWS MY LOVE AND HOW MUCH I CARE...
THE SADNESS IN HIS HEART REACHES MINE...
SO, OUT OF BED, I SLOWLY CLIMB...
THE YEARS HAVE REACHED BOTH HE AND I...
LIFTING ONE PAW AND THEN THE OTHER...
I GIVE A BIG HEAVE, A VERY GOOD TRY...
THEN BLUE'S ON MY BED AND UNDER HIS COVER...
WE COZY UP, TWO FRIENDS TOGETHER...
I FEEL HIS COMFORT UNDER MY ARM...
AND KISS HIS HEAD, I CHERISH HIS CHARM...
WE DRIFT OFF TO SLEEP
AND DREAM OF THE DAY...
WHEN WE WERE BOTH YOUNG...
AND I COULD WALK AND HE COULD PLAY.

"A Muchness of
Love"
Maureen

ABOUT THE AUTHOR

By Daniel Jon Kostalnick, M.D.

Maureen married her high school sweetheart, Chuck, and lives in California in the East Bay region of the San Francisco Bay Area. She has dedicated her life to her family, and to working with multi-handicapped children as a Sign Language Interpreter for the Deaf.

Maureen is widely recognized as an advocate for children with disabilities and those children who are forgotten.

CPSIA information can be obtained at www.ICGtesting.com
Printed in the USA
BVOW04*0345310314

349205BV00001B/1/P